MAGORA

HOLLY O'FLANIGAN

MAGORA
THE GOLDEN MAPLE TREE

BOOK TWO

 MARC REMUS

MISTY MOON
BOOKS

First published 2016 by Misty Moon Books

Copyright © 2016 Marc Remus
Illustrations © 2016 Marc Remus

www.MarcRemus.com/author

Cover design and illustrations by Marc Remus
Designed and typeset by Marc Remus

Editor-in-Chief: Nancy Butts
Copy editor: Marlo Garnsworthy
Associate editor: Crystal Watanabe

Magora - Book 2 (2 of 6) - The Golden Maple Tree

Summary:
In her second adventure to the parallel world of Magora, twelve-year-old Holly O'Flanigan must find a cure for her dying friend and former blood-thirsty Unfinished, Ileana, and discovers the surprising truth about the disappearance of her neighbor Ms. Hubbleworth.

ISBN: 978-3-00-051993-2 (Paperback)
ISBN: 978-3-00-051994-9 (ebook)

*For Ileana, who lend one of the characters
her name and inspired me to write this
book during my days
in Honduras.*

CONTENTS

Missing
Ms. Hubbleworth

**When you paint, you create. When you write, you create.
When you imagine, you create. We create every day,
even when we fear we can't create anything anymore.**

J oline Hubbleworth has been missing for over a year,"
boomed a female voice from the widescreen TV in the
Smoralls' luxurious mansion. "But the police have not yet
found sufficient evidence to consider this case a crime.
Jonathan Hubbleworth, husband of the seventy-two-year-old
Donkleywoodian, stated today in an exclusive interview with
DonkTV News at 9 that he believes his wife must have been
either kidnapped or killed. He explained further that possible
suspects are plentiful because the missing person was not much
appreciated in Donkleywood."

"She sure wasn't," Holly mumbled to herself, hiding behind the white leather couch in her foster parents' living room. She pulled down the knitted cap she had been wearing all the time to keep her curls under control. Why did Ms. Hubbleworth have to be so nosy? Holly sighed. If the grumpy old woman hadn't followed her into the attic, none of this would have happened.

Unlike most people in Donkleywood, Holly knew exactly where Ms. Hubbleworth was, but she kept quiet because her foster parents, the Smoralls, would have locked her up in the attic if she told the truth. Nobody would have listened to a twelve-year-old anyhow.

A year ago, Holly had jumped into a fantasy painting that had been created by her grandfather, Nikolas. Ms. Hubbleworth had been sticking her nose where it didn't belong when she accidentally tripped into the same painting. Even if Holly told the authorities, nobody would believe that Ms. Hubbleworth was alive and currently teaching art in a magical world called Magora. Nobody would have believed Holly but three other children: Brian, Rufus, and Amanda. They had followed Holly into the painting and attended Cliffony, Academy of the Arts, for a full year. There, they had learned to paint with the help of magic.

"Strange sightings have been reported on a regular basis," continued the TV reporter.

Holly peeked out from behind the leather couch and glanced past the orangutan-like heads of Mr. Smorall and his daughter, Barb.

"Numerous witnesses have claimed that flying seahorses

the size of cats have been seen in Donkleywood over the past year," said the reporter. "The police call it mass hysteria. Nevertheless, we cannot discount the fact that over forty-five people have reported these creatures that are said to be hovering in thin air."

Holly pressed her hand over her mouth so she would not let out a sound. The seahorses were still on the loose. Holly knew that this was not mass hysteria. These creatures were the helpers of an evil creature called S.A. Lokin, the Duke of Cuspidor. In Magora, Holly had come face-to-face with him. She had found out that he was one of the so-called Unfinished, creatures that had not been completed by a master painter.

"DonkTV will have a special report on the seahorse sightings tomorrow night, right after the News at 9," said the reporter. "Please join us tomorrow for…"

Holly didn't hear the end of the sentence. She felt the dust behind the couch tickle her nose. Like a volcanic eruption, a loud sneeze shook her whole body. Three fuming faces turned her way.

"What are you doing down there, loser?" Barb asked.

Ms. Smorall's giant hawk-like nose turned red, and the color spread to her cheeks. She let out a high-pitched scream and yelled, "Out of here! I've told you a million times you're not allowed in the living room. Back to the attic right now!"

She jumped up from the leather recliner, leaped toward Holly, and grabbed her by the ear.

"Don't make such a fuss about it, hon," said Mr. Smorall. "Holly is not worth getting worked up about."

"She's not allowed in here, Herbert," said Ms. Smorall. "You know exactly what a troublemaker she is. Even her teachers know she's living in a fantasy world. Back at Donkleywood School she never focused on her work. All she did was scribble everywhere."

"They are not scribbles," said Holly. "They are drawings. I'm a good artist. I even won—"

Holly stopped in the middle of the sentence. She had won the title of "Best Artist" in Magora, but since Ms. Smorall did not know anything about that fantasy world, it would only make things worse if Holly let that slip.

Ms. Smorall's face turned red. "You are anything but an artist," she yelled.

"But hon, what if she has some talent?" Mr. Smorall asked.

Holly noticed sudden panic on Ms. Smorall's face. Nervously, she pushed Holly out of the living room.

To Holly's surprise, Ms. Smorall whispered in an almost caring tone, "You'd better go now." Then, she spun around and screeched, "Herbert, darling, how could you even think that Holly has a spark of talent? You know how bad she is in the arts."

Mr. Smorall grunted and turned back to the news. Ms. Smorall slammed the living room door shut.

A few more weeks and Holly would not have to listen to this anymore. She was going back to Magora for her second year of studies at Cliffony, Academy of the Arts.

She trudged down the hallway, thinking how it would be to have caring parents like everyone else. Occasionally, Ms. Smorall seemed friendly, but every time Mr. Smorall appeared

she started screaming and acted as if she hated Holly from the bottom of her heart. Mr. Smorall was less vocal, but that was exactly what drove Holly crazy. She could deal with Ms. Smorall's verbal and physical outbursts, but she couldn't deal with the fact that Mr. Smorall treated her as if she were invisible.

After the death of her parents, Holly had lived most of her life with Grandpa Nikolas. And since he had been like a father to her until he died in a horrible fire last year, she missed having a dad more than a mom. Holly sat down on the marble staircase and thought about some of her friends she had met in Magora. There was Ileana, a former Unfinished who had just been completed through blood donations, and Cookie, the shape-shifter, who took care of the kids in the living tree house where they stayed, Villa Nonesuch.

"I have to get back to Magora," she mumbled. Even though it wasn't the real world, it had become her home now, and Cookie, Villa Nonesuch, and Ileana were a much better family than the Smoralls.

A sizzling sound echoed through the hallway and interrupted Holly's thoughts. She snapped out of her daydream and jumped up. What was that? The sizzling echoed again. Holly tiptoed back down the hallway until she reached Mr. Smorall's office.

She had never set a foot in the office before because it was off limits to her. Not that she had ever wanted to go inside, but this time was different. The sizzling seemed familiar to Holly, but she could not remember where she had heard it before. Carefully, she opened the door. There was a massive desk in the middle of the wood-paneled office. On the left was a fireplace, and on the right were bookshelves filled with papers and ring binders. Behind the desk was an open window. It banged violently against the shelves.

Relieved, Holly went to the window and closed it. It was nothing but the wind.

With a decisive slam, the door flew shut behind her, and Holly felt hot breath on the back of her neck. She spun around and stared into four blazing red eyes.

"S-s-seahorses," stuttered Holly, tumbling backward.

The two seahorses were covered in rusted armor and had spiked needles on their tails. Holly knew they were not to be messed with.

At that precise moment, a humming filled the air. Out of the corner of her eye, Holly saw a bright light forming in the air in front of the fireplace. The seahorses flinched. The rectangle increased in size, and within seconds, an entrance had opened up.

"Jeepers. A gate," said Holly, gaping at the light-filled opening. "Someone is coming from Magora."

A *whoosh* indicated that someone was on the way. A bright flash of light exploded from the gate, and there in front of Holly was a huge creature, wrapped in a black hooded cloak.

Holly wanted to let out a scream, but the sound got stuck in her throat. She began to breathe heavily and stuttered, "C-c-cuspidor."

The hooded creature leaned forward menacingly. Holly slid down to the floor and squeezed her eyes shut. It was all over now.

Goodbye
Piddlehinton Street

Painting and writing are both products of creativity. Even though the two seem different, they are more similar than we think.

Holly felt a breath on her face. She had her eyes shut, but she knew that Cuspidor was standing right in front of her. Scenes from the fight with Cuspidor about two months ago flashed through Holly's mind. She saw how he had drained her blood through a thread of paint that hovered between her and his paintbrush. She saw how he had ripped open his black cloak and revealed himself as an Unfinished who consisted of nothing but pencil lines. Cuspidor had drained Holly's blood and it was not until then that she realized she was someone special, a Gindar, someone whose artistic talent was uncommon. Gindars could only drain the blood of their own kind, and that was what Cuspidor had done.

But what was being special good for now? At any moment, Cuspidor would drain her blood until she was dead.

Holly felt a cloak sliding over her shoulder.

"Are you all right?" said a voice. "You look a bit sick today."

"Look a bit sick?" repeated Holly, confused.

She opened one eye and peered at the hooded creature. The hood had been pulled down, and a beautiful Asian woman stared at her. A lotus made of bone was fused to her head and butterflies danced around it.

At that moment, the seahorses shot forward, ready to attack when the woman swung her brush. A thread of paint emerged from the tip and shot toward them. In a split second, the seahorses were surrounded by paint that whirled around and then solidified into ice that froze them solid. The ice block set itself down gently on the floor.

"Professor LePawnee," said Holly. "What are you doing here? I thought you were Cuspidor."

"I had to cloak myself," said Professor LePawnee, turning back to Holly. "It would really cause problems if people saw me here."

Professor LePawnee was the headmistress of Cliffony. She belonged to a species called Ledesmas, which housed butterflies in the bone lotuses on their heads and shared each other's minds via these insects flitting back and forth between their heads.

A sound echoed as if a wine glass had been gently pinged

with a spoon. Holly turned to the gate. It closed in front of her eyes, and the light that emanated from the gate vanished.

Professor LePawnee stared at the gate, looking irritated. Then, she searched her pockets as if she had just remembered something. "I should have planned that better. I can't believe I forgot it."

"Forgot what?" Holly asked.

"I had a miniature painting of Magora that would allow us to go back." She stopped searching her pocket and looked at Holly with wide eyes. "But I forgot. Now we are stuck." She tucked her paintbrush into one of the sleeves of her dress. "At least I caught the seahorses."

"Good," said Holly. "The seahorses have been all over the news. It was about time they got caught. But how are you going to get back now?"

"How are *we* going to get back now," LePawnee corrected her.

"What do you mean?" Holly asked, hoping that this would mean she could leave Donkleywood.

"You don't have to stay here for the rest of the summer vacation. You can come with me to Magora tonight."

Holly jumped up. She was thrilled to leave the Smoralls and not have to stay another month.

"Jeepers! You mean I can spend part of my vacation in Magora?"

LePawnee nodded.

"I'll get ready right away." Holly headed for the door.

"Don't get too excited," said Professor LePawnee. "There is a negative side to all of this."

"What do you mean?" Holly asked.

"I will explain everything later," said the professor. "First, get Brian, Rufus, and Amanda and meet me at the old barn in the sunflower field while I'll take these ice blocks over there. And I guess we'll need your Grandpa Nikolas' painting now that I forgot the miniature painting."

"No problem," said Holly, wondering what negative news she could expect.

She hopped over the ice block, flung the door open, and ran down the marble hallway.

When she reached the attic staircase, she kneeled down on the second step and pushed against a plank of wood. A secret cubbyhole opened. She had used it as storage for mementos from Grandpa Nikolas. Now it also served as a hiding place for her magic paintbrush and the canvas of Magora. Holly had found this painting in a secret attic and learned that she could open it by using the magic brush.

Holly pulled out the rolled-up painting, which she had carefully packed in brown paper. She pushed the plank back in place, raced upstairs to her room, sifted through her drawers, and took out her backpack. She smiled when she thought of Tenshi, who had spent endless hours inside it.

Tenshi was a cuddly, orange, koala-like creature that Holly had found together with the magic painting in a finely-carved chest. Over time he had become more of a close friend than a pet. He seemed to know Holly better than most people did, and at times, he almost seemed human.

"Tenshi is waiting for me," she said, tearing a page out of a notebook. Holly scribbled on the paper.

Dear Mr. and Ms. Smorall:
Rufus told me that students are needed to set up the classroom at boarding school. I am leaving now so I can help them. I will be back for next summer vacation.

She stopped a second and then added with a gr*in*,

I hope you won't miss me too much.
Holly

She folded the paper, placed the notebook and canvas in her backpack, swung it over her shoulder, and went down the staircase. Before closing the door, she taped the note on it. Then, she tiptoed down the hallway and stepped over the threshold of the mansion. The smell of roses tickled her nose while a fresh breeze caressed her face. She was free again.

THE GOLDEN MAPLE TREE

Findley's Astro Shop

Writing, painting, movies, computer games, and many other fields require creativity. Even though these fields seem to be so different, they all need the same spark of creative energy to function.

Holly bolted down Piddlehinton Street, veered into Papplewick Road, and turned into a dark alley. It was time to get Brian. Dim lamps on the gray houses lit her way. The alley was narrow at first but widened further along she went. At the end, she came to a halt. In front of her was a pink two-story building. Gardenias grew in red flowerboxes on the windowsills. The house stood out against the gray buildings around it because of its bright color. A sign covered half of the upper floor that read, "Findley's Astro Shop."

Holly hurled two pebbles against one of the windows. A

window on the second floor opened and the round face of a blonde woman appeared.

"Sorry, Ms. Findley," said Holly. "I thought Brian was there."

The woman smiled. "Come on up. Brian told me all about it."

"About what?" Holly asked, confused but Ms. Findley had already closed the window again.

Holly entered the psychic reading store. The entire shop was packed with candles and astrological objects. Dozens of mobiles with stars, moons, and suns hung from the ceiling, slowly turning from the smoke of the candles below.

"It's so exciting," squealed Ms. Findley, stumbling down the staircase. Her curly blonde hair bounced up and down under a colorful gypsy-like turban. A black, baggy dress covered with stars and moons tried unsuccessfully to hide the rings of fat around her waist.

"I can't believe all this about Magora," said Ms. Findley. "And all this excitement about Cuspidor and—"

"Wait a second," interrupted Holly. "How do you know about Magora?"

"I told her." Brian was standing on top of the staircase. He straightened his glasses on his nose. "Mom had a vision about Magora. So yesterday, she told me that she had called Brushdale Boarding School and found out that neither of us is going there. I just had to tell her the truth."

"And you believe us?" Holly asked, knowing the Smoralls would have fallen over laughing if she had told them this story.

"Of course I do," said Ms. Findley. "I wouldn't be called a psychic if I didn't."

"So what are you going to do now?" asked Holly, scared that Ms. Findley might go and tell everybody in Donkleywood about it.

"Don't worry. I can keep a secret," said Ms. Findley, smiling. "It's so exciting to go to a whole new world. I wish I could go, too."

Brian gave his mother a look as if they had discussed this issue many times before.

"All right, I'm not coming," she said. "But now you'd better get going."

"We're not going right now," Brian said.

"I think you are," Ms. Findley said.

"How do you know that?" Holly asked.

"I just know," said Ms. Findley, winking. "I'm a psychic."

"What's going on?" Brian asked, looking at Holly.

"Professor LePawnee is here, and she wants us to go back to Magora now," said Holly. "We're to meet her at the old barn."

"Holy smokes," said Brian. "Now? That's so cool. I can't wait to see Ileana, Cookie, Villa Nonesuch, and—" He stopped. "Maybe not Farouche, but everybody else."

Holly grimaced. She didn't want to see Professor Farouche again either; he was the most disliked instructor at Cliffony. He taught Unfinished Painting, a class that had caused Holly major trouble in the past.

"Everything is ready," said Ms. Findley, pulling out a backpack from behind a big astrological clock. "I packed for you this afternoon." She grinned.

Ms. Findley gave Brian a kiss on the cheek, hugged Holly, and led them out the door.

"You've got to get Amanda," Holly said to Brian. "I'll get Rufus, and we'll meet in half an hour at the barn."

"We'll be there," Brian said.

"Take good care," called Ms. Findley. "And behave. I'll be watching you in my crystal ball."

Holly darted back down the alley and followed Papplewick Road until she reached the local post office. Instead of knocking at the door, Holly hurled two pebbles at Rufus' window on the second floor in order not to disturb his parents. A freckled face with red hair appeared.

"Holly? It is already past 8 p.m." Rufus said. "What's going on?"

"We're going back to Magora," whispered Holly. "Professor LePawnee is here and she wants us to come back now."

"But why now?" asked Rufus. "Surely it can wait until tomorrow."

"No," said Holly. "She said we have to meet her at the old barn now."

"I will be down in a minute," muttered Rufus, closing the window.

Twenty minutes later, Rufus casually trotted out of the post office.

"Boy, a snail is a race car compared to you," said Holly. "I'm sure they're already waiting for us." She pulled Rufus by the sleeve. "Let's run."

A few minutes later, the two were scurrying through a

sunflower field. The full moon lit their way, and Holly could make out Brian and Professor LePawnee standing by the barn.

"What took you so long?" asked Brian when they reached the building.

"Can't you guess?" Holly replied.

"Our slowpoke took his time again," said a voice behind Brian. Amanda Heavenlock came out of the barn.

Holly's mouth dropped wide open. "What on earth are you wearing?" she asked.

Amanda used to have long hair and dress up in Barbie-like outfits but at the end of last school year, she had begun to wear less girly clothes and cut her hair to shoulder-length. This time, however, she had overdone it. Amanda was wearing a military combat outfit, cross-country boots, and had her hair tucked into a baseball cap. Although she was just a year older than Holly, she wore a lot of makeup, and her fingernails were painted bright red. It was an odd combination.

Amanda looked down at herself. "What's wrong with it? I just figured we're going on another adventure. So I prepared myself."

"We're not going to the jungle," said Holly. "Last year might have been a bit eventful, but we didn't need military uniforms. And I don't think we will need them this year either."

"I don't think it will be as relaxed as you expect," interrupted Professor LePawnee. "We have a big problem."

"What kind of problem?" Holly asked.

But LePawnee just took the painting of Magora from Holly and went inside the barn. She unrolled it and swung her paintbrush. Paint shot out from the tip, encircled the painting, and within a few seconds had turned into a lake of shining lights.

"Ileana is severely ill," LePawnee said.

Just as the professor stepped into the lights she added, "If we don't do something soon, she will die."

With a *pop*, she disappeared.

The Beauty Parlor

I used to believe that painting works under different rules than writing, a different creation process. But it doesn't.

Holly stood frozen in front of the lights shining from the painting. Her friend Ileana was dying? How could that be? She had been healthy when they left Magora. Did it have anything to do with her being a former Unfinished, or did she have an accident?

"Let's go!" Brian said before leaping into the painting.

"Come on, Holly," said Amanda. "We have to find out what happened to Ileana."

Amanda pulled Rufus with her into the entrance and *pop pop*, they were gone.

Holly snapped out of her frozen position and stepped

into the lake. She zoomed down a tunnel of lights that danced around her like fireflies. It felt like going down a water slide. Suddenly, Holly saw an opening ahead of her. Assuming she would fall onto a grassy hill, as she had last time, she prepared herself for a soft landing. But this time was different.

"Watch out, Holly. It's a street," Brian's voice echoed through the tunnel as she fell down toward cobblestones.

Like a cat, she instinctively turned in the air and landed safely on her feet. Rufus and Amanda, however, didn't seem to have landed that skillfully. Both had grazes on their arms.

Holly stared up the cobblestone street that wound its way up the hill.

"Papplewick Street," Holly said, staring at the narrow street lined with crooked fairytale-style buildings that hosted all kinds of shops. It was packed with people. Among the crowd were dwarves and Ledesmas.

Last year Holly had strolled along this street many times and enjoyed the fantastic stores that offered any art supply and magical object she could have ever wished for.

Professor LePawnee was headed up to the castle that towered over the old buildings. Holly raced ahead so she would catch up to her.

"What is wrong with Ileana?" Holly asked.

"She is very sick."

"What does she have?"

"You have to see for yourself," said LePawnee. "Just follow me to the infirmary."

Holly's friends caught up.

"If Ileana is sick, what can we possibly do?" asked Brian.

THE GOLDEN MAPLE TREE

"She needs doctors, not us."

"Maybe she just needs our moral support," said Rufus from behind.

"Or maybe she'd like me to do her hair," said Amanda, skipping from one display window to the other, stopping longer at Wrinkle Dimple Skin Care Shop.

"You're really out of line, Amanda," said Brian. "Ileana is really sick. Don't you get it?"

Amanda's head drooped. "I'm sorry. I just thought that a little makeover might cheer her up."

Holly saw the bakery ahead of them in a shingle-covered building. Immediately she recalled what Ileana really liked.

"Could you please wait a moment?" Holly called up the street to Professor LePawnee.

The professor stopped and waited.

Holly went up to the window of the bakery. Last year Ileana and Holly had bought pastries in this bakery. Back then, they had found a miniature display of the island of Magora in the window, but this time there was something different.

"The Gallery of Wonders," said Holly. Her mouth dropped wide open and she immediately glued her forehead to the window.

She remembered the collection of magical gate paintings that they had discovered last time they were in Magora. What was in front of her now was an exact reproduction of that gallery in miniature size. Licorice strings were holding up paintings made out of dough while the double helix staircase in the center was made out of dark chocolate.

The door of the bakery opened and a familiar "Howdy"

bawled across the street. It was the dwarf who had sold Holly and Ileana pastries last year. "Take this, Holly," he said. "I heard about Ileana. I'm sure she would like it." He handed her a brown bag.

"How do you know my name?" Holly asked.

"Everybody knows who you are," said the dwarf. "By the way, my name is Chester."

Curiously, Holly peeked into the brown bag and found a few marzipan griffins. She was about to thank the dwarf when a screech sounded behind her. Holly spun around. Amanda stood in front of a shop, her mouth wide open as if she had swallowed a bug.

"What's wrong?" Holly asked.

Amanda pointed at the sign above the door. "Sashisatsoo's Beauty Parlor," it read in bold letters.

"Someone stole my idea," shouted Amanda. "Didn't I tell you that a beauty parlor would do well in Magora? Didn't I say so?"

Amanda shook Holly by the shoulders. Her face was red. She looked so angry that Holly thought she might start spouting steam from her ears and nose like a tea kettle.

Holly didn't understand how Amanda could make such a big fuss about someone stealing her idea at a time like this. Ileana was ill and Cuspidor was still out there. They had bigger things to worry about.

"Thieves!" screamed Amanda. She stormed toward the shop. Before she could bolt inside, the door opened and an eerie-looking woman stepped out. Her face was completely covered with scales, and a tail peeked out from underneath

her long black velvet gown. Her similarity to a snake was undeniable. Her pupils contracted as she hissed, "Is there a problem?"

Amanda came to an abrupt halt in front of the snake woman. "Are you the one who stole my idea? I wanted to open a beauty parlor."

The woman laughed and hissed again, "I don't think you have a patent on opening a shop like this, but if you are really interested to learn who had the idea—" The snake woman glanced over her shoulder to the stairs in the beauty parlor's dark interior. "Sweetie, would you come down for a second?"

A girl emerged from the gloomy interior. Holly's heart tightened to a knot and she felt anger rushing through her whole body when sunlight illuminated the girl's face.

"G-g-gina?" Holly stammered.

THE GOLDEN MAPLE TREE

The Chandrills

When painting a character, I have to show him with colors. When writing about a character, I have to show him with words.

Gina Chillingham had been Holly's worst nightmare ever since she had come to Magora. With her bully friend, Lismahoon, Gina terrorized every student at Cliffony.

"What are you doing here?" Holly asked.

"I live here," said Gina, grinning calmly.

Holly pushed Amanda behind her. Now that she realized Gina had something to do with it, Holly knew she had to take sides, even though she did not consider a beauty parlor worth a fight.

"You stole Amanda's idea." Holly leaned forward until she was nose-to-nose with Gina.

"I can do whatever I want," said Gina. She looked Amanda up and down and pointed at her. "Did you burn your hair with a torch? What a ditz!"

"Short hair is fashionable you, you, you—" shrieked Amanda and pointed at the woman. "Do you live with this snake?"

"She is not a snake," replied Gina. "This is my mother, Sashisatsoo. And if you don't leave now, my father is going to get you."

"Is your father a snake like your mother?" Holly asked.

"At least I have parents. Where are your yours?" Gina asked.

Holly felt her chest tighten in a knot and she started breathing heavily. Gina knew that Holly's parents had died when she was a baby. There was nothing Holly could say back to her.

"You scaly piece of scum," Amanda said. "Better to have dead parents than a mother who looks like a mutant and a father who doesn't show himself, probably because he doesn't want to have anything to do with you."

Sashisatsoo hissed as Amanda pushed Holly aside and grabbed Gina by the collar of her shirt.

"Stop that now," said Professor LePawnee, pulling Amanda and Gina apart. "This is no time for personal differences."

Holly didn't listen to Professor LePawnee. She stared into the window of the beauty parlor. Gina had hit a nerve. Ms. Smorall had never been a mother to her, and Mr. Smorall hardly ever noticed her. Grandpa Nikolas had been the closest thing to a father that she ever had. But now he was dead.

Holly would never know what it was like to have loving parents. At that precise moment, she thought she saw the reflection of her foster mother in the window. But how could that be? There was no way Ms. Smorall could be in Magora. Holly spun around and saw a woman disappear into a side street.

"Ms. Smorall?" Holly shouted, running after her.

Brian held her back. "Are you going bonkers?"

"But I saw her. I know it was—"

"Enough now," interrupted Professor LePawnee. "We'd better continue."

Holly followed the professor up the street, occasionally glancing over her shoulder at the side street where the woman who looked so much like her foster mother had just disappeared. But Ms. Smorall didn't know anything about Magora; she couldn't have come here. Holly must have been mistaken, that's all there was to it.

Brian interrupted Holly's thoughts. "I wonder what kind of creature Gina's mother is."

"Sashisatsoo is a Hissler," said Rufus. "I read about them in the Encyclopedia of Magora."

"What's a Hissler?" Brian asked.

"It is a creature that looks like a person with snake characteristics," explained Rufus. "I read that, hundreds of years ago, they were considered dangerous and were kept out of Magora. Over the centuries, however, they became relatively friendly and some mixed with humans. Gina must be a mix between a Hissler and a human. She does not have the snake-like looks, but she still hisses."

"What human would want to marry a Hissler?" Brian asked. "They're so ugly."

"Gina's mother must have found someone, or Gina would not be what she is," Rufus said.

As they passed the magic bookstore, Holly's attention was drawn to a large sign in the window. Hung over a display of dozens of copies of the same book, the sign read,

Butterfly & Gindar Holly O'Flanigan.
Read about the notoriously famous Ledesma, Butterfly,
and her defeat by Gindar Holly.

Holly was horrified. She wished she could hide in the ground like a mole. Being a Gindar placed her in the limelight already, but a book about her would certainly not help her keep any privacy.

"I forgot to tell you," said Professor LePawnee. "Professor Farouche wrote down his experiences about last year's events at school and had lots of success with the publication."

Holly scowled. Not only was Farouche the reason she had ended up face-to-face with Cuspidor, Farouche had also made Holly's life miserable ever since they met. And now, after all this, he had actually profited from her duel with Cuspidor.

"Come on, Holly," said Professor LePawnee. "We're almost there."

A few minutes later, they reached the wide courtyard of Cliffony between the towering walls of the castle. Last spring she had won the Quadrennial Art Competition right on this very spot. Holly stared up into the sky and remembered the

bats that had formed a canopy over the courtyard. This time, however, what looked like a flock of green birds fluttered toward them.

"I've never seen parrots here before," said Holly. "Isn't it too cold for them to live here?"

Professor LePawnee abruptly stopped and glanced horror-struck at the green swarm in the distance. "Those aren't parrots. Those are Chandrills." She began to walk a little faster.

"What are Chandrills?" Holly asked.

"Chandrills are a kind of flying plant," Professor LePawnee said.

"They don't look like plants," Holly said.

"Because they are not," said LePawnee. "They look like birds, but they are actually made out of leaves from blossoms."

"I don't understand," Holly said.

"They come from the Golden Maple Tree. Every spring the tree produces tiny flowers. They get bigger until they free themselves from the branches. Then, they fly around like the ones over there." LePawnee pointed at the swarm of Chandrills in the distance. "When winter comes, they change their color from green to red, just like regular leaves, and decompose until next spring when everything starts all over again."

"And what is the Golden Maple Tree?" Brian asked.

"It's a very special tree," explained Professor LePawnee. "The regular leaves are said to heal any illness."

"Where is this maple?" Rufus asked.

"According to legend, it is in the land of Cuspidor. Monks guarded the Golden Maple Tree and cut the flowers that become the Chandrills. Cuspidor took over the land and over time, the location was forgotten."

"So you think the flowers are no longer cut because Cuspidor did something to the monks?" Rufus asked.

"Exactly," said LePawnee. "Now the Chandrills can develop freely."

Holly glanced up into the sky. The Chandrills approached rapidly.

"It looks as if they are headed toward us," LePawnee said. "I think we'd better get out of the courtyard. Chandrills can be very aggressive and are quick to attack."

"But they can't get through the Wall of Gors," Holly said.

"Oh yes, they can," said Professor LePawnee. "The Wall of Gors destroys only the minds of animals and people, not plants."

"Jeepers, they're fast!" Holly shouted as she noticed the Chandrills circling above the courtyard.

Professor LePawnee began to run toward the Tower of the Bats. "Follow me now," she shouted. "They have seen us or they would not be circling."

Holly and her friends ran as fast as they could after the professor, but could not keep up. Suddenly, Holly saw a swarm of Chandrills swoop down on LePawnee. They buried their sharp beaks in her bone lotus. She screamed and tumbled to the ground.

"Get away," shouted Holly, trying to disperse the Chandrills, but a second swarm swooped down on her, too. She flung her hands up in the air and screamed. Briefly looking over her shoulder, she realized that nobody could help her. Brian, Rufus, and Amanda were encircled by what looked like a green

tornado.

Holly felt a sharp pain on her neck and screamed. A Chandrill had drilled its beak deep into her skin. Then, hundreds of Chandrills swooped down on her like vultures about to engulf a corpse.

Holly stumbled and fell to the ground. She would never reach the safety of the castle. Dizzy, she closed her eyes and tried to shield herself as best she could.

Ileana in Danger

A painting of a character gives the viewer no freedom to change the looks, but you can imagine what the person might look like on the inside.
A book describes things, but doesn't show pictures. It gives more freedom to the viewer to imagine what the person looks like from outside, but less what is inside.

Holly was lying on the ground, swinging her hands above her head to disperse the swarm of Chandrills. Surprisingly, they actually gave way. The pecking, biting, and pinching ended as suddenly as it had begun.

Holly opened her eyes.

The Chandrills were swooping back up into the sky, pursued by a swarm of bats. Every second, one of the bats buried its teeth into a Chandrill's body. With a painful screech, the Chandrill fell apart into leaves that sailed down to the ground.

In just two minutes, the courtyard looked as if a giant tree had shed its leaves everywhere.

"Are you okay?" asked a familiar voice from above.

Professor Gobeli, the Projectile Brushstrokes teacher, was looking down from a window in the Tower of Bats.

"I think I'm okay," said Holly as she watched her friends get up.

"I believe everybody is all right, Damaris," Professor LePawnee shouted up to Gobeli. "We've got to do something about this plague."

"The Chandrills seem to be increasing in number," Professor Gobeli called down. "Not long until my bats will be outnumbered. We'll be in big trouble soon."

"I will set up a meeting so we can discuss the issue," said LePawnee. She turned to the children. "But now we'd better go to the infirmary. I think we all need some treatment, and Ileana is waiting there, too."

Holly and her friends followed Professor LePawnee into one of the buildings, up the stairs, and down a white corridor. Flowers in clay pots were neatly placed on shelves along the walls. Light bulbs dangled above them.

Holly was painfully reminded of the time she had been in the infirmary. She had not followed the instructions correctly when using Mind-Splitting Powder, a powder that separated the mind from the body. Her mind and those of her friends had been caught in plants. It had taken their whole Christmas vacation to get out of them.

"This is Professor Hubbleworth's entire first-year class," said LePawnee, pointing at the line of flowerpots.

Holly gulped.

"Holy smokes. What happened?" Brian asked.

"Professor Hubbleworth was on a field trip with her class," explained LePawnee. "They had a picnic and she offered the class tea, but accidentally mixed up the sugar and MSP tins. Needless to say, the result was devastating."

Professor LePawnee urged them on. They continued through another corridor until they reached a door. It was tightly shut with three locks and numerous bolts, as if a serial killer was being kept inside. The sign on the door read, "Ileana Kennicott."

"Why has she been locked up like this?" Holly asked.

"We had to. You will see for yourself," replied Professor LePawnee.

At that precise moment, a sound like a tiger's growl echoed from inside the locked room.

"Be careful," said a calm voice behind them.

Holly spun around and looked into the face of an old man with long white hair and bushy eyebrows. He pulled down his reading glasses.

"Ileana is not what you expect her to be," said Professor Kaplin as he reached under his white cloak for a keychain.

As he unlocked the bolts and inserted the key, the growling stopped. The professor opened the entrance to a dark room. Holly couldn't see a thing. Only the light from the hallway allowed her to see the outline of a bed at the far end of the room.

"Take your time," said Professor LePawnee. "Your eyes will adjust."

Holly stepped inside, clinging to the paintbrush in her pocket in case she needed it.

Ileana was tied to the bed. Thick leather belts restricted her movement entirely. Her eyes were closed. The smooth pale skin she once had was no longer. Holes the size of walnuts covered her cheeks and neck. The blanket underneath her head was visible through the holes. It was as if she were dissolving. Of her former beauty only her long brown hair remained, as well as her body.

"She's changing back to an Unfinished again," said Holly as she sat down on the bed, rubbing her eyes to hide the tears that were forming. "How can that happen?" She touched Ileana's half-dissolved hand.

Ileana shook violently, and her eyes sprang open. Holly stared into two empty holes. Like a wolf caught in a trap, Ileana wrestled underneath the leather belts. With an eerie growl, she grabbed Holly's hand and sank her nails into her palm.

Holly cried out. It was not only the pain in her hand that shocked her, but also the knowledge that one of her best friends was turning into a monster. Holly struggled to free herself without success. She stared into Ileana's face, but couldn't see anything that reminded her of her friend.

Professor Kaplin leaped to the window and pulled a curtain just an inch to the side. A ray of light reached Ileana. She winced and released Holly's hand just as the professor closed the curtain again. Brian, Rufus, and Amanda dashed to the bed.

"Are you okay?" Brian asked.

Holly nodded. "What happened? Why is she an Unfinished

again?" She looked at the professor, wiping the tears off her cheeks with the back of her bloody hand.

"We don't really know," said LePawnee. "Ileana has a disease that causes her blood to dissolve. She has lost so much blood that she's returned to an Unfinished state."

"But can't you give her new blood?" asked Brian, stepping closer to Holly and putting his arm around her.

"We have tried so often, but every time we give her a transfusion the blood destabilizes within hours and she dissolves again." LePawnee sighed heavily.

"Unfortunately, we can't waste any more blood on her. We can better use our blood reserves to heal other Unfinished."

"But there must be something we can do," Holly said.

"There may be one chance," said Professor Kaplin. "That's why we needed you to come here, Holly."

"What is it?" Holly asked.

"Gindar blood might help her," said LePawnee, "because it can be given to any Unfinished without being rejected. So maybe it will help her. And you are a Gindar."

Holly didn't have to think about it. "Let's do it," she said. "We don't have time to lose."

Professor Kaplin clapped his hands, and two nurses came in, pushing another bed for Holly inside. One of the nurses set up a transparent tent around Ileana's bed. Then, Kaplin opened the curtains, making the room more pleasant.

"Stop," Holly shouted as she jumped forward to the curtain and closed it again. "Ileana will die if you let the light in."

Kaplin smiled. "Don't worry," he said. "This tent is not transparent from the inside. Ileana can't see anything but outlines. It keeps her in the dark so she won't dissolve in the sunlight like an Unfinished would."

Holly relaxed and opened the curtain again. "So we can be outside of the tent in the light and Ileana is still safe," said Holly. "That makes it nicer to be in here."

"You might have to stay here a while," Professor LePawnee warned.

Kaplin nodded. "We don't want to take too much blood at once. Just a little every day so that you don't weaken too much."

"I guess I should make myself comfortable then," said Holly, taking off her shoes and lying down on the bed next to Ileana's. "Let's get started."

"But first let me heal your wounds," said Kaplin. "It looks like all of you have suffered a Chandrill attack."

Professor LePawnee nodded as Kaplin swung his brush over the children. Bright light radiated toward them. Holly felt as if she were on a beach during the hottest time of the day. At first, it was as if the sun were burning her skin. Then suddenly a breeze blew and a tingling sensation filled her whole body. She looked at her wounds. They had disappeared, as if they had never existed.

"Now let's get started," Professor Kaplin said.

The Robin

Painting and writing make characters come alive. How real can a character become? Can a fictitious character become part of the real world?

For the next couple of weeks, Holly spent most of her time in the infirmary. Once a day, the nurses took Holly's blood and injected it into Ileana's veins. Even though Holly felt weak after each transfusion, she was determined to continue. Between worrying about losing her friend and the blood donations, she used the time to practice her brushstrokes and talk to her friends, who visited her frequently.

After a while, the therapy seemed to pay off. Some of Ileana's holes had disappeared, and Ileana looked more human than before. Holly was really happy and felt relieved that she could start school without having to worry about her friend.

One morning, the door to the infirmary room flew open and Brian, Rufus, and Amanda bolted in, holding neatly-wrapped presents in their hands. "Happy birthday!" they shouted.

Holly sat up in bed. She had almost forgotten her birthday. In the past few weeks, she had only thought of Ileana.

"We got you some presents," Rufus said.

"And we brought you someone," whispered Brian. "I know animals are not allowed in the infirmary, but I just sneaked him in."

A koala-like creature peeked out of the backpack that Brian was carrying.

"Tenshi," said Holly, excited. She hadn't seen the Nukimai all summer long.

"And there is someone else who wants to see you," said Amanda, nodding in the direction of the door.

A llama-like animal trotted in, its long tongue swinging from left to right like the pendulum of a grandfather clock. A robin was sitting on its back.

"What on earth is that?" Holly asked, laughing.

"It's a Slamee," said Amanda, grinning.

Holly shrugged.

The llama-like creature suddenly grabbed the robin with its tongue and sat it on the floor. Then the Slamee spun in circles and turned into a tornado. On top of the tornado a troll's head popped out.

"Cookie," Holly laughed. "You're a basket case."

The tornado turned into the body of a huge troll.

"Wasn't that a dramatic entrance?" Cookie asked, picking up the robin and placing it on his shoulder.

"Very dramatic," said a voice behind the shape-shifter. Professor LePawnee came in. "Happy birthday."

Holly hopped out of bed. She jumped at Cookie and landed right in his outstretched arms. "Thank you," Holly said to LePawnee.

"You don't know how much I missed you," Cookie said.

"And I missed you," replied Holly, kissing him on his big nose.

"But wait," said the troll, setting Holly on the floor. "I have a surprise for you. There is someone who will keep you company while you are in here."

Cookie stomped out the door and came back holding an elongated box in his hand. The robin sat on top of it.

"What a cute bird," Holly said.

"Oh no," said Cookie, grabbing the robin with one hand and placing it back on his shoulder. "He's not the present. I just found him at the Wall of Gors. The Gors caught him and extracted his mind from his body. He's basically dead unless another mind enters him."

At that precise moment, Ileana moaned briefly, and then fell silent. The robin on Cookie's shoulder shook violently, shot up into the air, and began to spin in circles above their heads.

"Out of here," shouted Professor LePawnee, pushing everybody toward the door. "He's going to attack us."

The robin swooped and came directly at the professor. LePawnee aimed her brush and paint hit the bird. Within a split second, an ice block formed around the robin and froze it in mid-flight. The block set down gently on the ground. Ileana moaned loudly.

"Jeepers. What on earth was that?" asked Holly, turning away from Ileana to Professor LePawnee.

"It was Ileana," said Rufus. "I have read in the *Encyclopedia of Magora* that an Unfinished can take possession of an empty body, provided the body to be possessed has been emptied of a mind before. Unfinished humans can enter any type of body; unfinished animals usually can only enter animal bodies."

Professor LePawnee nodded. "Ileana's mind was in that robin a minute ago. In Unfinished Painting II you will learn all about what Unfinished can do."

Holly was shaken by the attack. She could not believe that her friend Ileana would not recognize her.

While the nurses connected Ileana to some tubes that provided her with blood, Cookie handed Holly the parcel. "Now back to your present," he said.

Still horrified by what had just happened, Holly opened the box and found a gnarled birch branch inside.

Cookie grinned at her. "What do you think?"

"Why are you giving me a piece of wood?" Holly asked, confused.

Amanda rolled her eyes. "What a stupid present," she said.

"It's not just a piece of wood," said Cookie. "Take it out of the box."

Holly sat the box on her bed and grabbed the branch. It was no longer than a paintbrush, but as thick as a cucumber.

"My dear, please be a little gentler," hollered a voice.

"Who said that?" asked Holly, surprised.

"I said it." The branch in Holly's hands shook. "Happy

birthday, my dear. I thought I would keep you company."

Holly recognized the voice. Astonished, she turned the branch in her hand.

"Villa Nonesuch? Is that you?" she asked.

On the other side was a blue eye and a pair of thick wooden lips.

"Of course it's me, my dear," the mouth said. "Since you couldn't come to see me, I asked Cookie to bring a piece of me to you. It took a while to grow these eyes and lips, and it hurt quite a bit when he broke off that branch, but for you I would do anything."

"This is so cool," said Holly. "Now we can take you wherever we go, and you don't have to wait to hear our stories." Holly smiled. "You know what?" she said. "I think Amanda should carry Villa Nonesuch."

Holly knew that Amanda didn't get along too well with the tree house. This was a chance for the two to get to know each other better.

"Me?" cried Amanda, backing away from the bed. "That tree house doesn't like me, and I don't want to carry her with me all the time."

"And that's exactly why," said Holly. "Maybe if you spend more time together you will get along."

"What a lovely idea," Cookie said.

"Come on, Amanda," said Holly. "Please take her. It's my birthday."

Reluctantly, Amanda took the branch. "Okay. But only because it's your birthday."

"Don't hold me so tightly," Villa Nonesuch shrieked.

"I'm not," Amanda protested.

"Yes, you are."

"No, I'm not. Shut up, you stupid branch," said Amanda, stuffing it in her pocket.

"Stop it!" said Brian. He turned to Holly. "Thanks. Now we have to listen to this all day."

"Perhaps," added Rufus. "And now we have a mother who is looking over our shoulder all the time."

All of a sudden Holly heard a weak "Happy birthday" behind her.

She turned around. Ileana had propped herself up in bed. She was no longer staring at Holly through two black holes. Her brown eyes glittered brilliantly, just as they used to do.

"Jeepers. It's finally working! The blood helped you," said Holly as she closed the curtains and pulled up one side of the tent. She stepped inside and untied Ileana's body. They hugged each other hard while tears of joy rolled down Ileana's cheeks.

Professor Kaplin left the room, shouting across the corridor, "Ileana has recovered."

"We thought we had lost you," Holly said.

"I'm not giving up that easily," Ileana said, smiling.

At that moment, the door to the room flew open and a tall, skinny boy about fifteen years old came bolting in. His wavy black hair was tied back in a ponytail, and numerous medals were attached to his neatly-kept school uniform, as if he were a high-ranking military officer.

"Illy, my sweet Illy is back," he shouted.

"My brother Calvin," Ileana said, rolling her eyes.

Seemingly unaware of the people around him, Calvin ran

through the room and fell into Ileana's arms, burying his head on her chest, sobbing, "You're back, my sweetest sister."

"Ahem," Rufus said and cleared his throat twice.

Calvin stopped sobbing. A few seconds of uncomfortable silence passed. Then he lifted his head and looked around. It was as if lightning had struck him. He released Ileana abruptly, staring at the other kids as if he had been caught in one of the most embarrassing moments of his life. He stood up and said in a composed manner, "Well, it was about time you recovered."

Nobody said anything. Calvin stammered a few more words, but was rescued only when a handsome boy appeared at the door. He was tall, and his face reminded Holly of a model she had seen in a fashion magazine in Donkleywood. The boy glanced at Holly, smiling. Holly felt heat rushing to her face. She quickly turned away, knowing she must be blushing.

"So how is your sister doing?" the boy asked.

"Fine," Calvin said with a relived smile. "May I introduce you to Marvin?" he pointed at the handsome boy. "He's my new assistant for organizing the annual Christmas party. We're in the same class."

Marvin stepped into the vault and greeted everybody. After he had shaken hands with Professor LePawnee and Cookie, he approached Holly.

"And who are you?" Marvin asked.

Holly opened her mouth, but nothing came out. She opened and closed her lips, like a fish blowing bubbles.

He waited with his hand outstretched, beaming at her with vivid blue eyes.

"This is Holly," Amanda said, pushing herself in front of Holly and batting her eyelashes. "But more importantly, I haven't introduced myself yet. I'm Amanda Heavenlock." She grabbed Marvin's hand and shook it with both of hers. "What a pleasure to meet you. If you have some time, we could—"

"Could I have a word with you?" interrupted a voice coming from Amanda's bag.

"Not now," whispered Amanda.

"Now," Villa Nonesuch said.

"This is not the right time," Amanda said.

A big grin stole over Brian's face. "Maybe it was not such a bad idea after all to have Amanda take care of Villa Nonesuch," he said.

"Yes, this might teach her some manners," Rufus added.

But before anybody could say another word, a growl interrupted the conversation. Ileana was squatting on her bed like a monkey about to pounce. Her eyes had turned back into two black holes. Growling, she swung her upper body back and forth.

"Everybody out of here," shouted LePawnee. "She's had a relapse."

The crowd stumbled out of the room. Holly remained, rubbing a tear from her cheeks. Just a moment ago she had her friend back, and now she was facing a monster again. Holly realized that she was trembling.

"Ileana. It's me," Holly said. "Don't you remember me?"

"Get out of there. Now!" shouted Professor Kaplin as Ileana leaped straight at Holly.

Return to
Villa Nonesuch

**Can a real person become part of a fantasy world?
I believe he can, because in the mind anything is
possible. Fantasy is only a facet of reality.**

Holly darted toward the door, but Ileana caught her ankle
and pulled her back, like a lion dragging its prey.

"Leave her alone," shouted Marvin, grabbing Holly's hand.

Holly clung to Marvin as Ileana pulled with all her
strength.

"Help us!" Marvin yelled.

Brian sprang forward and took Marvin's hand, while
Professor LePawnee took her paintbrush and created a bright

thread of paint that shot toward the curtains at the window. It pulled them a few inches aside and let sunlight stream into the room. Ileana squealed, released Holly's ankle, and crawled back to her bed.

Professor LePawnee swung her paintbrush once more, and a lilac thread of paint penetrated the transparent tent. It lifted up the leather belts and flung them around Ileana. She thrashed about wildly, fighting the belts, but they restrained her within seconds.

LePawnee stepped back into the infirmary room, trailed by the others.

Holly lay on the floor, still holding Marvin's hand. Embarrassed, she pulled it back and stammered, "Th-th-thank you, Marvin."

Professor Kaplin trudged to Ileana's bed. "I just don't understand this disease. It's like a black hole that eats up everything. Once we have replenished her blood, it starts dissolving again. I thought that Gindar blood might help but—"

"Obviously it didn't," Holly interrupted. She got back up on her feet. "My blood is not good for anything. Maybe I'm not a Gindar after all."

All the time and blood she had sacrificed had not helped Ileana one bit.

"What will happen to her if this doesn't stop?" Holly asked.

"If the dissolution of the blood cells continues at this rate—" Professor Kaplin hesitated for a moment, "—she will die."

There was a moment of complete silence. Holly felt as if an invisible hand was penetrating her chest, grabbing her heart, and slowly squeezing it like an orange.

"But there must be some way to help her," Brian said.

Professor Kaplin shook his head and turned around.

"I'll find a cure," Holly said.

She did not want to give up hope for her friend even though she had no idea what to do. Holly stormed out of the infirmary and left Cliffony, trailed by her friends.

However, her mood improved a bit when she saw Whitespot sitting on the stairs next to another maroon-colored griffin.

"You brought Whitespot with you?" Holly asked.

"Of course we did," Brian said. "We've been staying in Villa Nonesuch. How do you think we got here today?"

Holly ran down the stairs. Whitespot squawked with delight when he saw her. She flung her arms around his neck and petted the white spot on his forehead.

"No stopping," yelled a voice from behind. Mr. Hickenbottom, the janitor, had appeared at the gate. He pushed up his thick horn-rimmed glasses. "I have told you hundreds of times that griffins are not allowed to stop here." He ran down the stairs, his long purple cloak floating behind him. "If everybody does what he wants, we might as well open a griffin parking lot up here. Land your griffin down at the marketplace next time, or I will inform the authorities."

"Oh, relax," interrupted Cookie. "This was an emergency."

Mr. Hickenbottom glanced, disgusted, at Cookie. "Trolls. I'm not talking to trolls."

"I'm sorry, Mr. Hickenbottom," said Holly. "Ileana is sick, and they had to get here quickly. I assure you it won't happen again."

The janitor grunted and watched carefully as Holly, Brian, and Amanda climbed up on Whitespot. Rufus and Cookie took the other griffin.

The shape-shifter clapped his hands. "Time to go back home."

The griffins swung themselves up, and in an instant, they were high in the sky, leaving behind the maze of towers.

It was a joyful return when Holly arrived at the Griffin Hatchery. She was warmly welcomed by Villa Nonesuch. Her room inside the large tree house was cozy and comfortable, just as she had left it. Finally, she was home again.

Over the following weeks, Holly tried to learn all kinds of healing brushstrokes that might help cure Ileana, but nothing really worked. After a while she didn't know anything else to try, so she kept staring out of the window, watching baby griffins learn how to fly, while thinking about how she could help Ileana.

The Wednesday before school started, Holly and Brian were silently sitting in their rocking chairs on the patio that overlooked the lush meadow with Lake Santima in the distance. Beyond the lake, the Land of Cuspidor lay behind a veil of mist. With the black clouds above, it appeared threatening as always.

Holly remembered her fight with Cuspidor beneath the lake. She wondered if he had died down there when the cave was flooded. But even though she didn't hear his voice in her mind anymore, she had the nasty feeling that he was still alive.

"Have you studied the curriculum yet?" Rufus broke the silence as he came out onto the patio with a piece of parchment.

"School hasn't even started yet," said Brian. "Why bother till we get the schedules on Monday?"

Holly nodded.

"Your grades are not exactly exemplary," Rufus said, turning to Brian. "And yours are just average," he said to Holly.

Brian rolled his eyes, grunted in disapproval, and leaned back in his rocking chair.

"I have checked out six books on Unfinished Painting I, three books on Creation and Deletion, and five books on Projectile Brushstrokes," said Rufus. "I am sure this year I will get top marks in all the classes. I might not be as talented as you two, but studying can make all the difference. Studying is one of the essential pillars…"

Rufus' voice grew softer and fainter until it disappeared, even though he was standing right next to Holly. She just couldn't pay attention to what he was saying anymore. Her mind was going full speed, thinking about how she might help Ileana. There were more important things in life than studying, and Ileana's life was definitely one of them. What could she do to help her? Was there still hope?

Holly was distracted by something far in the distance, on the other side of Lake Santima. A large creature was galloping along a meadow on the bank of the lake. Holly leaned forward in her rocking chair and squinted. Was that a giraffe? A radiant green one? Holly jumped up and her rocking chair banged against the wall.

Rufus stopped talking.

"What's wrong?" Brian asked.

"Look! Over there." Holly pointed toward the creature.

Brian rummaged in his pocket and fished out his glasses. "Let me see," he said as he put them on. "That's a giraffe."

"Thanks, Brian, I wouldn't have been able to see that for myself," said Holly. "But why is it green?"

"Isn't it lovely?" Amanda squealed, bolting out of the tree house. "I saw it yesterday. Wouldn't that shade of green look just marvelous as nail polish?"

Rufus briefly glanced at the animal and said, "It is not a giraffe—it is a swarm of flies."

Holly, Brian, and Amanda stared at him. Holly was confused. Was Rufus making fun of them?

"What do you mean? That's obviously not a swarm of flies," Brian said.

Rufus sighed. "If you had read the book I suggested earlier, you would have learned about the many species that exist in Magora."

"Do you think we're stupid and can't tell the difference between a mammal and an insect?" Holly asked.

"Well, they are not exactly flies," said Rufus. "They are Giraflies."

The Giraflies

When painting a place, I have to show things visually. When writing about a place, I have to show things verbally.

"What on earth are Giraflies?" Holly asked.

"They are flies with bright green eyes," said Rufus. "They live in large communities and group themselves together in the form of giraffes each time dangerous animals are in sight. Giraffes don't have natural predators. Giraflies know this and camouflage themselves this way so they are safe from birds, bats, frogs, and other predators. The green of their eyes is so strong that when they get together the giraffe appears green."

"And what is that?" asked Brian, pointing at a large flock of birds fluttering from the land of Cuspidor toward the island.

"Chandrills." Holly gulped. "They really are becoming

pests."

The Chandrills headed right past the Giraflies. As they whizzed by, something unexpected happened. Like a sandcastle falling apart into millions of grains, the giraffe dissolved from the head down. In a split second, it turned into a green swarm of flies that dashed after the Chandrills and cut them off. The bird-like creatures tried to veer around, but the Giraflies merged with them and suddenly disappeared.

"Jeepers," said Holly. "What happened? Where are the Giraflies?" She looked at Rufus, hoping for an answer, but he just shrugged.

The Chandrills continued toward the island and past the Wall of Gors. As soon as they had crossed, the Giraflies emerged out of nowhere and assembled back into a giraffe right on the lawn in front of Villa Nonesuch.

"This is incredible," said Holly. "The Giraflies have a way to pass the Wall of Gors without having their minds separated from their bodies."

"That's correct," said Villa Nonesuch. "They are not just like ordinary flies. They have realized that they can only find a way to get to the island if they hide their minds. Chandrills are known to be mindless creatures because they consist solely of leaves. Inside they are empty."

"But the Chandrills seem to know where they are going," said Holly. "They don't seem to be *that* mindless."

"As a collective they aren't," said Villa Nonesuch. "The individuals have so little mind that the Gors don't recognize it. But as a swarm they are able to think like very basic animals. And Giraflies seem to know that they are empty, and so they enter the Chandrills and remain inside until they have passed the Gors."

"So the Gors can be fooled?" Brian asked.

"I guess so," replied Villa Nonesuch. "Even Gors are not perfect."

"So there are more ways into Magora than just using gate paintings and MSP," said Holly. "What if someone crosses the Wall of Gors by hiding in a Chandrill?"

Cookie peeked around the patio, followed by three baby griffins on a leash. He laughed. "Nobody can hide inside a Chandrill, except maybe a Q person. They are the only ones who are small enough to fit in a Chandrill."

Suddenly, the griffins squawked in agitation, tore themselves away, and bolted toward the green giraffe that trotted along the meadow. The Giraflies continued, unimpressed.

"Get back here. Now!" Cookie shouted as he ran after them.

The baby griffins swung themselves up into the air and for an instant, their outlines seemed blurred. Suddenly, they started spitting fire.

"Don't you dare," shouted the shape-shifter, angrily. "That's it."

He spun around like a tornado and changed into a black dragon with a spiked tail. The baby griffins approached the Giraflies. Like a house of cards falling apart, the giraffe dissolved and spread about in all directions. The dragon shot up above the baby griffins, plummeted down like a stone, and cut off the griffins' path. With his spiked tail, he forced them back to the ground.

A miniature tornado whirled around the dragon, and a second later Cookie was back in his old shape.

"Don't you three ever do that again, or I will send you to the mines," Cookie said.

He picked up the leashes and pulled them back to the patio.

"Sorry about this interruption. They still don't know what they are allowed to do and what not."

"I did not know that griffins could spit fire," Rufus said.

"They can't," said the troll, nervously.

"But they just did," Rufus insisted.

"They didn't," said Cookie, trying to avoid Rufus' intense glance.

"But we saw it," Brian said.

"Everything took place so fast. You probably just saw some fog," explained Cookie, trotting away quickly toward one of the barns. "Well, no time to talk. I have to go and lock them up. See you in a bit."

"He is hiding something," Rufus said.

Holly and Brian nodded.

At that precise moment, a tiny red Chandrill came fluttering toward them. It was much smaller than the average Chandrill, and its bright red color distinguished it from the others. It shot with precision through the branches of Villa Nonesuch and plummeted toward the patio. Everybody dropped to the ground, expecting an attack. But to their surprise, the Chandrill landed gently on Rufus' head. Everybody got back up.

"What do you have there?" Holly asked, pulling out a photo from the Chandrill's beak.

It was a photo of a small library no bigger than a room. Holly didn't recognize any of the books on the shelves, but there was nothing out of the ordinary about the place. Rufus slipped the photo into the *Encyclopedia of Magora*.

"So what kind of bird is this?" Amanda asked.

The bird hopped onto Rufus' shoulder, chirping joyfully.

"It certainly looks like a Chandrill," said Rufus, stroking the leaves of the creature.

"It might not be one if it is so friendly," Amanda said. "They usually bite."

Rufus held out his index finger and the Chandrill hopped onto it. "This one shows no sign of aggression."

"I wouldn't trust it if I were you," Brian said.

"I think I want to keep it," Rufus said, smiling.

"I don't know about that," said Holly. "It still seems to be a Chandrill. But that's up to you."

"Do you want to give it a name?" Amanda asked.

"Shardee," said Rufus promptly. "I once had a bird with that name, and my mother gave it away."

"Okay, it's Shardee," said Holly, smiling. She sat back down in her rocking chair and stared at Cuspidor's castle, which had appeared from behind the fog in the distance. "Since Shardee is a Chandrill, maybe he can show us the way to the Golden Maple Tree."

"Why do you want to go there?" Rufus asked.

"Remember that Professor LePawnee said the Golden Maple Tree has healing powers?" Holly asked.

Her friends nodded.

"If we find the tree, we might have a cure for Ileana and

be able to stop the Chandrill attacks at the same time," Holly said.

"You're right," said Brian, as he sat down on the stool. "I didn't think of that."

"The tree is just a legend, and the Chandrills might come from somewhere else," said Rufus. "Nobody knows for sure."

"Of course we'll have to do some research," Holly said. "And find out more about what the tree can do."

"Why don't we start at the library?" Brian asked.

Rufus sighed loudly. "Forget about it. I have done that already. I have checked every single book that exists in Cliffony's library. There is nothing about that tree."

"There must be something. Maybe if we—" Holly stopped in the middle of her sentence. She had heard a murmur somewhere in the distance. "Did you hear that?"

"Hear what?" Amanda asked.

The unintelligible murmur came closer and then suddenly it was very clear to hear.

Holly jumped up from the rocking chair. She ran from one end of the patio to the other. Then she stopped at the railing and turned to her friends.

"Cuspidor is back," she said.

The Momarian Hell Library

Writing about places gives you more freedom to imagine. Painting places provides more details at one glance, but it cannot stimulate the same senses that writing can.

Brian and Amanda jumped up from their stools. Rufus seemed paralyzed. They all stared at Holly in disbelief.

"You can hear Cuspidor again?" Amanda asked.

Holly nodded. The Unfinished's raspy voice started repeating itself.

Where are you Holly? Cuspidor boomed.

But then it ceased and mixed with another voice that was somewhat familiar to Holly.

"You haven't checked the Momarian Hell Library yet."

This second voice was not coming from within Holly's mind. It was coming from outside. From the stunned expressions on the others' faces, Holly knew someone was standing behind her. She spun around.

The brim of a giant sunhat decorated with pencils and paint tubes almost poked Holly in the eye. Ms. Hubbleworth was leaning over the railing of the patio.

"Jeepers, you scared the heck out of me," Holly said.

"You haven't checked the Momarian Hell Library yet," Ms. Hubbleworth repeated.

"What are you talking about?" Holly asked.

"You were wondering where you could find the Golden Maple Tree," Ms. Hubbleworth said.

"Have you been eavesdropping on our conversation?" Brian asked.

Ms. Hubbleworth nodded. "Go and search the Momarian Hell Library," she said a third time.

"I have read about that library," said Rufus, "but there seems to be no reference to where the library is located."

"You'll find it," said Ms. Hubbleworth and chuckled briefly.

Holly watched as the professor climbed onto a black griffin that came out from behind Villa Nonesuch.

"School orientation will start on Friday. Be there at eight o'clock sharp," Ms. Hubbleworth shouted as she took off into the sky.

"She is eerie," said Rufus. "She spies on us, gives us a hint where to check for information on the Golden Maple Tree, and then she takes off."

"She's not eerie. She's a nutcase," said Brian. "That's all she is."

"So you've read about this Momarian Hell Library?" Holly asked.

Rufus nodded. "But I could not find out where it is."

"There is one place that nobody dares to mention," Holly said.

"You mean Ravenscraig Lane?" Amanda asked.

Last school year, they had explored this rundown alley and discovered that it was filled with shops for those who worked with the more sinister arts.

"Cookie might know if the library is in Ravenscraig Alley," Brian said.

The four dashed to the barn where Cookie had disappeared a few moments earlier. They knocked. The gate opened a few inches, and the troll peered out. "What do you want?"

"Can we ask you a question?" Holly asked.

Cookie raised an eyebrow.

"It's not about the griffins," said Holly. "I just want to make sure that Momarian Hell Library is at 25 Ravenscraig Lane."

"No, it is at 86 Ravenscraig Lane," said the shape-shifter. "Wait—how do you know it's on Ravenscraig Lane at all?"

"We didn't. Until now," said Holly with a big grin. "Thanks, Cookie."

The four ran back to Villa Nonesuch.

"Ravenscraig Lane is no place for you to be," shouted Cookie behind them. "It's not open to students until fourth year."

But Holly wasn't listening to him. She was already thinking

of a plan to get into Ravenscraig Lane. The entrance to the alley was on Papplewick Street. A giant guarded the entrance. Last school year, they had been able to get in because the giant had left for a few moments. This time it would be more difficult. School was about to start, and Papplewick Street was probably filled with students getting their supplies. The giant would pay extra attention in order to keep them out.

Holly dropped into one of the comfortable recliners in the living room of Villa Nonesuch.

"Tonight we are going to Ravenscraig Lane," she said. "At night fewer people are watching."

"Yes," chirped Amanda. "The adventure is about to begin!"

"We do not have a password," said Rufus. "And by the way, in case you do not remember, last time we entered that street we ended up in the infirmary as plants."

"Yes, but we can't worry about that," said Holly. "Ileana's life is in danger. We can't let her down."

Disapprovingly, Rufus stomped his feet on the ground. Then he went up to his room.

"I'll wake you up when we're ready," Holly called after him.

After the moon had risen high in the sky, Holly felt a jolt on her shoulder. Brian was shaking her. She had fallen asleep in the recliner.

"We better get going now," whispered Brian. "Whitespot is ready."

"Why are you whispering?" asked Holly. "Amanda and Rufus are coming, too."

"We don't want to wake up Villa Nonesuch. She's asleep."

Amanda paraded down the staircase as if she were presenting the latest fashion. "I'm ready," she announced proudly. In addition to the military outfit and boots she had started wearing this year, Amanda had added a helmet covered with twigs.

Holly imagined herself wearing such a helmet instead of her knitted cap. She laughed. "You look funny," she said.

"Where do you think we're headed—the forest?" Brian asked Amanda.

"Who knows?" said Amanda. "Last time we ended up in a tropical greenhouse, remember?"

Brian rolled his eyes. "Sure," he said and put on his sweater.

They sneaked out of the tree house, climbed onto Whitespot, and flew off. A few minutes later, they were standing on Papplewick Street. Not a single person was out. Only the giant leaned against one of the crooked buildings on the corner of Ravenscraig Lane. His eyes were closed and he snored loudly.

"And what now?" asked Brian. "How are we supposed to pass him?"

"He's asleep," said Holly. "If we're careful, we can pass without him noticing us."

Rufus hesitated, but Brian pushed him forward.

"This is not a good idea," Rufus said.

They tiptoed past the giant's feet and passed the corner of Ravenscraig Lane without a problem.

A few moments later, they stole along the dark alley, hiding in the shadow of the dull, gray facades. In the daytime, light barely penetrated the alley, making it hard to see, but at night the darkness was absolute, almost as if someone had blindfolded them.

They passed a few shops and reached the ward where the Unfinished were kept. Holly was painfully reminded of the bad conditions inside. She sighed, but pressed on. The alley took a bend to the right and widened. The buildings increased in size, but their dilapidated state didn't improve. Never before had they ventured so deep into Ravenscraig Lane.

"I think we should go back," Rufus said.

"Don't start that again," said Holly, while Amanda gave him a friendly slap on the back of his head.

The street opened up farther and ended in a large square surrounded by monumental Roman-style buildings. The buildings were in disrepair, and the square was covered with rubble, as if it had lain abandoned for many years.

Only a few people, dressed in black, crossed the square. Nobody paid attention to the four kids.

"I guess we found it," said Holly, pointing at a large building. It looked like a Roman temple with columns on the front and a towering spire above. A wide staircase led up to three double doors that had a sign reading, "Momarian Hell Library."

Holly was about to head to the library when Brian suddenly darted in the opposite direction.

"Where are you going?" Holly asked.

"My mother is here," Brian said.

"Has he gone bonkers?" Amanda asked.

A few moments later, Brian came back. "I saw my

mom down the alley, but she disappeared into one of the buildings."

"Your mother is in Donkleywood," Rufus reminded him. "You made a mistake."

"I did not," said Brian. "You think I wouldn't recognize my own mother?"

"It is dark and you probably did not see correctly," Rufus said. "Your sight is not the best anyhow." He pointed at Brian's glasses.

Brian protested, "I know what I saw and—"

"You are not supposed to be in Ravenscraig Lane," said a voice, coming from Amanda's direction.

They all turned toward Amanda but no one was there but her. She stood frozen in fear.

"You are getting yourself into trouble," said the voice.

Amanda grimaced. "I forgot to leave Villa Nonesuch's branch at home." She pulled the branch out of her backpack.

"You snuck out while I was asleep," it said. "Did you think I wouldn't find out?"

"Please, Villa Nonesuch," said Holly. "We need to get into the library and find information about the Golden Maple Tree to save Ileana."

The eye on the branch blinked a few times. "Okay, this time I didn't see a thing, but next time I won't tolerate such behavior." The eye closed.

Holly went to the library's entrance and found it open. Inside a large entrance hall was a wooden desk with a leprechaun behind it. His face was covered with oozing warts and he was reading a newspaper.

"Weebit, could you come over and help me for a moment," a voice sounded through the hall.

The leprechaun left the hall through a door behind the desk. "I'm coming," he shouted.

"Perfect timing. This is easier than I thought," said Holly as she tiptoed through the hall. Her friends trailed after her. She pushed the stained-glass door to the library open. Nobody was inside, but thousands of books filled the shelves around a circular room. They reached high up into the spire. Staircases crisscrossed the room, allowing visitors to reach even the highest shelf.

Hours later, they had checked virtually every inch of the library. Holly had found books about black magic, werewolves, and vampires. But there was nothing on the Golden Maple Tree.

"So what now?" Brian asked.

"I guess we have to go home," said Holly, looking at the sunbeams falling through the windows high up in the spire. "The sun is up already."

They hurried back toward Ravenscraig Lane. Holly was crushed that they hadn't been successful. Ileana might die because they could not find out where the Golden Maple Tree was.

Patwood Alley

A well-written or well-painted place of a fantasy world can become part of reality. Once you have entered this magic place, you start wondering if reality is actually fantasy.

In frustration, Holly kicked a stone. An "ouch" echoed through the alley. Holly had hit someone. She dashed to the boy lying crouched on the street holding his ankle. Her friends followed.

"I am so sorry," said Holly. "Are you all right?"

"Don't worry, I—" The boy looked up from his ankle.

"Marvin," Holly burst out. "What are you doing here?"

"Getting knocked over by pretty girls." Marvin grinned at her. Then, his smile vanished. "Seriously, you have to hide now. Farouche is in there." He pointed at a shop filled with paint cans.

"Why are you here with Farouche?" Amanda asked.

"I'm his personal assistant," said Marvin, noticeably irritated. "Farouche caught me a few months ago when I stole into Ravenscraig Lane. He gave me detention, and now I have to help him with his chores. But what are you doing here?"

"We're trying to help Ileana." Holly offered Marvin a hand to get up. "We've been looking for a book on the Golden Maple Tree, but without success."

"Have you checked Patwood Bookstore?" Marvin asked.

Brian stepped up to him. "If there's no information in the Momarian Hell Library, we wouldn't find anything in a bookstore, would we?"

"Patwood specializes in books that the library does not carry. It's just around the corner in Patwood Alley." Marvin pointed at narrow little side street a few houses down.

"Watch out, Farouche is coming!" Rufus said as he jumped behind some garbage bins.

Holly glanced briefly at the window of the store and saw the professor leaving the counter with a large packet and a few paint cans.

"See you, Marvin," said Holly as she leaped behind the garbage bins just as the door of the paint supply store flew open. Brian and Amanda followed her.

"Get over here and help me carry this," Farouche barked at Marvin.

Marvin picked up the paint cans and followed the professor down the alley.

"Next stop, Patwood Bookstore," Brian said.

"It is already 8:30 a.m.," said Rufus. "The streets will be busy soon. We have to get out of here, or some of the

professors might see us."

"Just a quick look," said Holly, peering around the corner into Patwood Alley. "I can see it. The bookstore is right over there."

A three-story building leaned precariously over the alley as if it were about to collapse. Garbage was piled up in front of the windows of the other stores. Only a narrow path led through the garbage to the shop.

"Let us go home," said Rufus, fidgeting.

A hissing suddenly caught their attention. A boy around Holly's age stepped out from behind a gutted couch. His body was covered in scales, and a long tail trailed behind him.

"I work for Patwood," he said. "Are you looking for anything in particular?"

"Let us get out of here," whispered Rufus. "It is a Hissler."

"Yes, actually, we are looking for a book," Holly said.

"Do not tell him what we are doing here," said Rufus through clenched teeth. "I would not trust him."

"But he might know something," Holly whispered. "I'm not going to let this chance go by." She turned back to the Hissler boy. "We are looking for a book on the Golden Maple Tree."

"A rare book to be looking for," he said. "I think I may have something."

The Hissler disappeared behind the couch, and a few moments later reappeared with an old book. It was bound in something that looked like snakeskin. The title was embossed on the front. It read, "Healing Medicine from the Golden

Maple Tree."

Holly stepped forward eagerly and reached for the book, but the Hissler pulled it away. "You don't think it's free, do you? It will cost you 20 Q."

Holly pulled out her pouch and chose a large golden cube. "20 Q. Here it is," she said, handing it over.

"You have not even looked at the book," whispered Rufus. "It might be a fraud."

"Would you shut up for one second?" whispered Amanda. "This might be our only way to find out about the tree."

The Hissler took the golden cube, searched in his pocket, and pulled out a tiny silver cube. "For you, it's 10 Q." He smiled and handed Holly the book and 10 Q.

"I guess Hisslers aren't so bad after all. Fifty percent is quite a discount," Holly whispered to Rufus, wondering why the Hissler was so generous for no reason.

When she turned back to the Hissler to thank him, he had already vanished.

"So let's see what this book tells us," she said as she strolled out of Patwood Alley.

"Holly O'Flanigan," echoed a voice. "What are you and your friends doing here?"

Holly looked up from the book cover. Farouche was standing in front of her, his lips trembling with anger.

"We were ju-ju-just…" stuttered Holly until she gave up trying to find an excuse. A tense silence hung in the air for a few seconds until Marvin stumbled toward them, the paint cans still piled up to his chin.

"I asked them to come and help carry the paint cans," said

Marvin. "Here, take them." He dropped a few paint cans into Brian and Rufus' arms.

"You asked them to come without my permission?" Farouche growled. "Detention. Every single one of you." Farouche grabbed Holly by the ear. "And what is this?" He snatched the book out of Holly's hands.

"We need that!" Holly yelled.

"Confiscated," said Farouche. "Monday, you'll have detention." He turned to Marvin. "And you, Mr. Armand, will remain my assistant for the rest of the year."

Marvin sighed. His head drooped as they all followed Farouche out of Ravenscraig Lane.

"I'm so sorry," Holly whispered to Marvin. "You didn't have to do that."

"I know," said Marvin, smiling. "But I wanted to."

Holly felt heat rushing up to her head. She quickly turned away, knowing she must be blushing again.

Monday morning, Holly woke up to find Tenshi bouncing up and down on her belly as if it were a trampoline. She'd had a terrible night because she was constantly dreaming about how she got Marvin into trouble.

"Wake up," Villa Nonesuch interrupted her thoughts. "Everybody is waiting for you."

"What time is it?" Holly sat upright.

"Seven thirty," replied Villa Nonesuch. "I tried to wake you before, but you didn't budge until I asked Tenshi to take care of it."

"Jeepers, I'm late!" She jumped out of bed, quickly brushed her teeth, and put on some clothes. Then she dashed down the stairs.

"We have been waiting for ten minutes now," Rufus said reproachfully. They were already sitting on Whitespot's back. "We are going to be late because of you."

"Sorry," mumbled Holly as she climbed on Whitespot.

It took only a few minutes until Cliffony's turrets came into sight. They approached the giant gate. Holly watched the first-year students entering and remembered that last school year she had met Ileana there, right on the stairs. And this year, Ileana might die because Holly hadn't been quick enough to hide the book from Farouche.

Whitespot landed gently in front of the gate. The students had already entered Cliffony and nobody was outside anymore.

"No stopping. No stopping." Mr. Hickenbottom had stormed down the staircase and was trying to scare Whitespot away with some frantic hand gestures.

"He'll be gone in a second," said Holly as she dismounted Whitespot.

"It's always you, Ms. O'Flanigan. You never follow the rules," shouted Mr. Hickenbottom. "I'll report you next time."

"He says that every time," said Brian as he got off the griffin.

Holly sent Whitespot off to the market square and a few moments later, they had entered the Grand Hall. They had missed the selection process in which the first years were asked to create some kind of painting with their magic brushes after consulting the oracle Gullveig.

LePawnee was standing behind one of the large tables and was introducing the instructors.

Professor Farouche was sitting next to LePawnee. In front of him was a book. Holly immediately recognized the snakeskin cover. It was the book she had bought from the Hissler.

"I'll get that book back," Holly whispered.

"I'm sure Farouche will keep it locked up in his office," Rufus said.

"No problem," Holly said. "We just have to remind Farouche that we have detention today, and he'll lock us in his office."

"Not a bad idea," said Amanda. "Then we have all the time in the world to search for the book."

Holly nodded. "Provided he doesn't carry it around with him all the time."

Professor LePawnee finished the introduction of the instructors and told the students that Gobeli had the schedules ready in the Tower of Bats.

"Let's get out of here before everybody else does," said Holly. "I don't want to stand in line."

They raced through Bristle Brush Hallway, turned a few corners, and reached the Tower of Bats. The rusty metal door was open. In the dim candlelight, Professor Gobeli rummaged through an ornately-decorated silver box. Holly was surprised not to find any bats flying around.

"Where are the bats?" she asked.

"They are too busy with the Chandrills," said Professor Gobeli, looking up from the box. "Those creatures are becoming a serious problem." She pulled out a few parchments from the silver box. "Here are your schedules."

Rufus picked up his schedule and opened it. "Aqua-inking?" he muttered. "I do not want to aquaink. That is nothing for a sophisticated student like me. It is a stupid class."

"What is it?" Brian asked.

"You will like it," replied Rufus. "It is a dirty, brutal, and unrefined sport that has been in practice for centuries."

"Cool," Brian said. "Come on, let's go and eat lunch."

"I'll pass," said Amanda. "I'm not really hungry."

Holly nodded, thinking that Amanda was so much thinner than her already.

Brian and Rufus took off down the staircase, while Holly and Amanda unrolled their schedules.

"Gate Paintings II with Ms. Hubbleworth," Holly read aloud. "Have you heard of Professor Kasmera? She's our instructor for Color Painting I."

Amanda unrolled her parchment. "I have never heard of her before, but I'm sure it'll be a fun class. Finally, I'll learn to create colors for nail polish—" She hesitated and looked up from the parchment with a satisfied smile, "or even body glitter."

"I'm sure Brian would love that," Holly teased.

Holly thanked Professor Gobeli, and they left the room. "I'm wondering if Ms. Hubbleworth can make up the time we lost last year," she said as she walked down the stairs.

Last school year, they hadn't been able to learn much in Gate Painting I because Cuspidor had stolen the paintings that led to other worlds. Ms. Hubbleworth hadn't even taught the class, but Professor Winney, the faun, had taken over and allowed them to use the class period to do other things.

Still immersed in her schedule, Holly missed the first step, lost her balance, landed hard on her butt, and whooshed down the steep staircase. The parchment flew through the air.

"Help!" she shouted, as she tried to hold on to the railing.

The crowd on the base of the stairs dispersed rapidly. Only one boy didn't seem to hear her. He turned just in time for Holly to knock him over.

The Book

A well-written description about a fantasy world can become real for the reader.

"M-m-marvin?" stuttered Holly. "You again? Are you okay?"

"I'm fine. What about you?" Marvin asked, just as Amanda came running down the stairs.

"Everything all right?" Amanda asked.

Holly nodded as a Ledesma boy helped Holly up.

"Thanks, Billy," said Holly, rubbing her legs. They felt a bit bruised, but she was not hurting too much. "Sorry, Marvin. I slipped," she said and stretched out her hand.

Marvin grabbed it and pulled himself up.

"This is not the first time you've knocked me off my feet," he said, winking at her.

The crowd burst out in laughter. Holly knew she had to be blushing again.

She was embarrassed and did not want the whole school to know that she liked Marvin. Annoyed, she turned to the crowd and snapped, "Mind your own business! I don't even like him. Now would you let me through?" Holly pushed a few first years aside. She glanced back over her shoulder at Marvin as she walked down the hallway. His eyes were no longer beaming with excitement; they looked droopy, like those of a cocker spaniel.

Holly felt bad for what she had said, but with all the people gathered there was no way she was going to go back and apologize.

She turned back around and ran right into Professor Farouche. "I'm sorry," said Holly, looking up at him.

"Good to find you here, Ms. O'Flanigan. You don't think I forgot your detention, do you?"

There wasn't much chance of that, Holly thought. In fact, she was going to remind him if he had forgotten. "Are you going to lock me up in your office?" She couldn't help but smile, thinking of her book as she said this.

Farouche grabbed her arm and dragged her back to the crowd of children. "And you, Ms. Heavenlock, are coming, too." Farouche pointed at Amanda, bawled twice at the crowd of students, and pulled the two girls to a staircase leading to the basement where his office was located. "Marvin, follow me," he shouted.

When they reached the door, Farouche turned to Marvin. "Get the parchments I gave you this morning."

Marvin dashed off and returned a few minutes later with a towering stack of papers. As he dropped it on the desk, he slipped a folded piece of paper into Holly's pocket.

"All right. Copy the parchment," said Farouche. "Empty paper is on the shelves. I'll be back to check on you."

He pushed Marvin out and slammed the door shut. With a decisive click, the two girls were locked in.

Amanda grinned. "Just what we wanted. Get the feather out and let's have this parchment copied."

Holly pulled out a red feather with two ends from her backpack. Last year they had discovered that Grandpa Nikolas' feather was full of magic. Holly swung her paintbrush, made a brushstroke, and a thread of gray paint encircled the feather. It propped itself up and ink came out of its bottom. It began to write.

"That's done," said Holly. "So where do you think the book might be?"

"He might have put it among all the other books on the shelves," Amanda asked.

She searched the volumes, while Holly looked inside the closets. But the book about the Golden Maple Tree was nowhere to be found.

"By the way," asked Amanda, "what did Marvin give you?"

Holly showed Amanda the folded paper. "I don't know," she said. "It's probably an embarrassing note."

"Come on, he's really nice to you," Amanda said.

"I know he is," Holly said, plunging into Farouche's armchair behind the desk. "And that's what scares me. I might get too attached to people here. Because reality is reality and a painting is still a painting. Magora is a fantasy; it will never be real. And I don't think it's a good idea to start believing it ever could be."

"You're right," said Amanda. "But it all feels real, so we can at least enjoy the time we have here as long as it lasts."

Holly nodded while she unfolded Marvin's note. She smiled. "He really is nice."

"What did he write?" Amanda asked.

Holly read aloud. "Check the desk drawer. Farouche left the book in there."

Now Holly felt a bit guilty that she had rejected him in public. She leaned forward in the armchair and pulled on the drawer. It was locked.

"Wait a minute," said Amanda. "I always carry a hairpin. It comes in handy." She pulled it from her pocket.

"This is not a movie," said Holly. "You can't just open a drawer with that."

"Just watch me." Amanda stuck the pin into the keyhole and wiggled it back and forth. With a click, she opened the lock. "I used to open my mother's cosmetic bag to get her makeup," she said, grinning.

Holly pulled out the drawer and saw the book. "There it is. Marvin was right." She placed it on the desk and was about to open it when a bang on the door interrupted her. A key turned, and Marvin stormed in.

"Farouche is on his way back," he said, completely out of breath.

"Quick, let's put it back." Amanda leaned over the desk

and grabbed the book. But Holly held onto the other end. Like tug-of-war, the two girls pulled on each end.

"I'm not giving it back now," said Holly. "It's mine. I paid for it."

"Farouche will catch us," growled Amanda, pulling with all her strength on her end.

Holly pressed her knee against the desk to get a better hold. Amanda's hands slid off the book. With a thump, she landed on the floor.

"Let's get out of here, now," Holly said.

"You can't," said Marvin, looking down the passage. "He's already down the hallway."

"Put it back," demanded Amanda.

But Holly clung on to the book as if it were the only thing in her life she cared about.

At that precise moment, a crafty expression stole over Marvin's face. He grabbed one of the books on the shelves, pulled out his paintbrush, and made a brushstroke Holly had never seen before. The leather cover changed into snake skin and within a split second a replica was in front them. Marvin hurled the copy over to Amanda, who chucked it into the drawer and locked it with her hairpin. Amanda leaped to the table and grabbed the magic feather that was diligently copying the parchment.

"What are you doing at my desk?" growled Professor Farouche as he stepped into the office.

Hidden from sight behind the desk, Holly slid the book under her shirt behind her back. "There wasn't enough space on the table, so I thought I could do the work here."

Professor Farouche raised one of his eyebrows in disbelief, pushed Holly off the chair, and took out a bunch of keys. "I don't trust you." He unlocked the drawer, pulled out the replica of the book, and took it with him. "Let's go, Marvin."

"What's wrong with you?" Amanda swung her brush and made the feather continue its task. "Farouche almost caught us stealing."

"Sorry," said Holly. "I couldn't just let Ileana's last hope vanish. It was my grandfather who didn't finish her in the first place. So in a way I'm responsible for her life."

"So that's what all this is about?" asked Amanda. "You feel guilty that Grandpa Nikolas didn't finish the painting of Ileana?"

Holly sat down on the desk. "If he had been more responsible and finished all the Unfinished, we wouldn't have the problems we have now. It's up to me to make up for what Grandpa Nikolas has done wrong."

"It's not your responsibility to fix what he messed up," Amanda said.

Holly pulled the book out from underneath her sweater. "Maybe I can't finish everyone. But at least I want to help Ileana."

Amanda stared at the book. "So let's see if this can help us."

With a deep breath, Holly opened the old snakeskin cover.

Villa Nonesuch's Big News

A well-painted place in a fantasy world can pull the viewer inside and make him believe he is in another world.

Holly flipped through the book in disbelief. "This can't be true," she said.

Not a single letter was written on any of the wafer-thin pages. It was empty. Furiously, she hurled the book against the shelves. "I should have listened to Rufus. He said we shouldn't trust that Hissler."

"But why would the Hissler sell you an empty book?"

"Why?" Holly said bitterly. "Just to make money."

For hours, Holly and Amanda remained in silence. They

brooded on what they could do while the feather was working on the parchment.

It was late in the evening when the feather finally finished its task. After Professor Farouche checked on them, Holly dropped the pile of finished parchment in his arms and zoomed past him. Amanda followed.

Once they had returned to Villa Nonesuch, Holly slammed the door to her room shut, annoyed that the Hissler had deceived her. Villa Nonesuch gave a brief "ouch" but didn't complain.

In the middle of the night, Holly awoke. She felt her pulse pounding in her temples.

Holly, you will be mine, soon, Cuspidor's voice echoed in her mind.

"Don't start this on me again," she shouted toward the open window. Her fists were clenched. "I'm sick and tired of your threats. You will not get my blood again."

Holly pulled the blanket up to her nose and pressed a pillow over her head. A few moments later, she was asleep again.

The next days turned out to be quite uneventful. Holly used the time to read a few books. She was still angry that she had been so stupid to trust the Hissler and not even look inside the book before buying it. But since she couldn't change what had happened, she decided to learn some more brushstrokes.

On Saturday morning, Holly woke up to the pounding sound of rain against her window. She got dressed and walked downstairs to have breakfast.

Brian, Rufus, and Amanda were standing in their bathrobes around an empty table, looking confused.

"What's going on here?" asked Brian. "What happened to our breakfast?"

"Villa Nonesuch, are you angry with us?" Rufus asked.

No cupboard door flipped open, no table shook, and Villa Nonesuch's bright voice was nowhere to be heard.

"Villa Nonesuch, would you please let us know what is going on?" Rufus asked again.

"I guess she doesn't want to talk with us," said Holly, taking out the cereals from a cupboard. "She might be sleeping."

"I'm sure she can hear us," whispered Amanda. "Just let me take care of this." She stepped into the center of the living room and shouted, "Tree houses are pests: nothing but old rotten logs."

"Stop it," said Brian. "If she's mad at us, she's not going to react to your insults."

Holly nodded as Amanda sat down at the table. Everything was quiet.

"See? It didn't work," Brian said.

"Very strange," said Holly as she tapped on the cereal box. A few pieces of cereal in the shape of paint tubes hopped out of the box. They had tiny feet and arms and held onto each other as they jumped from the edge of the box down into the milk bowl. For a moment they played there, splashing at each other as if they were babies in a bathtub, but as soon as Holly dipped the spoon into the bowl, they became regular cereal again.

"I wonder if something might have happened to Villa Nonesuch," said Brian. "Last night my bed wasn't made, and she's not been cleaning the place well anymore."

Rufus nodded as he took Shardee off his shoulder and placed him on the chandelier above the kitchen table. "She is probably busy with something else." He spread some blackberry jam on a piece of bread. "Did I tell you that Shardee likes the same food I like?"

Holly didn't care what food the Chandrill ate. She walked to one of the worn leather recliners and placed the bowl of cereal on the floor next to her. Tenshi followed her, grabbed the bowl, and gobbled it down.

"Thanks, Tenshi," said Holly. "That was my breakfast. I fed you earlier already. Why do you always like to eat my food?"

Tenshi just rubbed himself on her leg and jumped up into her lap.

"I hope Villa Nonesuch is all right," Brian said.

"I think it's quite nice to have her shut up for a while," said Amanda as she sat on the carpet and began to paint her toenails. "The branch also has its eye closed."

"We will wait a while and see if she wakes up," said Rufus. "If she is not back by tonight, we will go and tell Cookie."

"And there he is," said Brian, pointing out the living room window.

Cookie was running across the meadow through the torrential rain that was now accompanied by thunder and lightning. There was a knock on the door.

"Come in," Brian called.

The shape-shifter flung the door open. "What a day. I'm drenched." He wiped a puddle of water off his bumpy, bald head. "I have to dry off." He whirled around as he always did when changing form, and turned into a hovering green towel.

The towel rotated rapidly in the air, catapulting water all around him.

"Stop it," Amanda scolded as water covered her from head to toe. "You are ruining my nail polish."

Cookie turned back into a dry troll.

"Amanda's right. You're making everything wet," said Holly, frowning as she wiped the water off her face.

"You'll be a lot wetter in a minute," said Cookie. "We are going out there now. I have to show you something important."

Holly propped herself up in the recliner. Was Cookie about to show them what he was doing in the barn? Or did he know why Villa Nonesuch was silent? She was curious enough to find out that she was willing to run through the pouring rain.

"Come, follow me," Cookie said.

They put on their raincoats and followed the troll outside, plodding through the mud alongside Villa Nonesuch's trunk.

"You might have noticed these past few days that Villa Nonesuch has not been as attentive as she used to be," Cookie shouted over his shoulder against the noise of the lashing rain. "I will now show you why."

A few moments later, they reached the back of the tree house. The branches hung low. The troll pushed them aside and vanished in the thicket.

Holly and her friends followed. Underneath the canopy of leaves, they were protected from the downpour. A small clearing opened up in front of them as Cookie pushed a few more branches aside.

"Jeepers," Holly cried out. "Tree house seedlings!"

Four tiny trees houses no larger than Holly herself were flipping their branches back and forth.

"They are scared of the storm," said Cookie. "Villa Nonesuch had them weeks ago, but she didn't tell you because you were too busy."

"Hello, my dears," echoed Villa Nonesuch's voice above them. "Glad you could come and see my babies."

"Congratulations," said Holly. "And I thought you were angry that we sneaked into Ravenscraig Lane."

"I haven't had time to worry about that," said Villa Nonesuch. "My dear, these babies are a handful, I tell you. I have been protecting them for weeks."

"From whom do you protect them?" Rufus asked.

Villa Nonesuch sighed. "The Chandrills. I cover my babies under my branches. Occasionally, I let the sun through, but I have to watch the skies all the time and be prepared when the Chandrills come."

"Ouch," yelped Amanda. She had stretched out her hand to one of the seedlings and been slapped right in the face by one of its branches.

"Just like their mother," she complained. "Nasty tree houses."

Amanda turned around and stomped back the way she had come.

"I guess she'll have four more problems now," Brian said, grinning.

The storm subsided, and Villa Nonesuch opened up her branches a bit. Rays of light penetrated the gray clouds. Holly squatted next to the tallest seedling. In the sunlight, she could

see its tiny door and windows in the trunk.

"They are so cute," Holly said.

"This is Villa Willy," said Villa Nonesuch. "He's growing really fast."

"But how can they grow big if they are so close to each other and with this little light?" Holly asked.

"That is where Cookie comes in," said Villa Nonesuch. "He will replant them in other places when they are big enough."

At that precise moment, they heard a squawking above. A swarm of Chandrills shot toward them as Villa Nonesuch tried to disperse them with her branches. Holly felt a painful peck on her head. She shrieked and thrust the bird against the trunk with both her hands. But more Chandrills followed until Holly was surrounded by them.

"Quick, inside!" Cookie yelled as he warded off a few of them. He pushed some branches aside and uncovered a small back door in Villa Nonesuch's trunk. Brian and Rufus sped inside, their arms flung over their heads.

"Come on, Holly," shouted Cookie as he squeezed himself into the tiny entrance. "You have to get inside the house, now!"

"I have to help them," Holly yelled, staring, panicked, at the scene in front of her.

The Chandrills were attacking Villa Willy and tearing him to shreds. Villa Nonesuch violently flung her branches at the creatures, trying to protect her children. She whizzed a branch after a Chandrill, missed it by a few inches, and hit Holly right in the face.

It knocked Holly backward off her feet. Her nose started

bleeding as the Chandrills pounced on her.

"Get off her!" yelled Cookie, speeding toward Holly. With his giant hands he squished a few Chandrills. Some of them let go of her for a moment and attacked the troll.

Lying on her back, Holly watched as more Chandrills swooped down on her from the sky. She felt dizzy and closed her eyes.

14

The Chandrill Attack

When painting an object I have to show texture, form, and material visually. When writing about an object I have to show it through words.

Blood dripped from Holly's nose down her chin.

It's over now, Cuspidor's voice suddenly echoed in her head.

She opened her eyes again.

"You are not going to get me," she said.

Holding her bloody nose, she staggered back up onto her feet. Briefly, she glanced upward, seeing hundreds of Chandrills covering the sky. Then she stumbled past Cookie toward Brian and Rufus, who were waiting inside the entrance to Villa Nonesuch.

"We got her," shouted Brian as he pulled Holly inside.

Cookie spun around like a tornado, shrank to a bullet, and shot back into the entrance, where he transformed back into a troll.

Brian released Holly and slammed the door shut. Rufus swung his brush over Holly's nose. The bleeding stopped. She slid down the wall and sat on the floor.

The squawking of the Chandrills increased, while the pecking at the door's tiny window didn't seem to stop. Then suddenly, the squawking ended and a deafening screech filled the air.

Brian and Rufus got up on their toes and peered out the window.

Holly pulled herself up and squeezed in between her two friends.

"What's happening?" Holly asked.

"No!" Brian hollered.

The Chandrills had covered the tree house seedlings. Villa Nonesuch was fighting them off in vain. The more Chandrills she smashed with her thick branches, the more swooped down from above. For a few more seconds, the seedlings screeched. Then they fell silent.

Holly pulled on the doorknob, trying to open it, but Cookie pressed hard against the door.

"Let me out. We have to help them," she said.

"There's nothing we can do," said Cookie. "It's too dangerous."

The Chandrills fluttered a few times past the door before they disappeared into the sky, leaving four mutilated tree houses behind. Holly darted outside. Villa Nonesuch was sobbing.

The seedlings were dead. Every branch had been ripped apart. Not a single leaf was left untouched. Holly caressed a slender trunk, but neither the eyes nor the lips opened.

"I hate Chandrills!" Holly sank to the ground and hammered her fists into the puddles, covering herself with a thin layer of mud. "I'll find the Golden Maple Tree and stop the Chandrills from reproducing."

"They are the nastiest creatures I've ever known," added Brian, then he turned and glared at Rufus. "And you are keeping one of them as pet."

Shardee fluttered up and landed on Rufus' shoulder. "He is not a Chandrill, or he would be aggressive like they are." He placed his hand over the creature's body as if he tried to protect him from Brian.

"He's a rotten Chandrill. That's all he is," yelled Brian, his face turning red.

"As long as he stays that friendly, I wouldn't worry," Holly said as she scratched Shardee's head. The creature twittered.

"I regret very much what just happened," said Rufus, "but I think you are prejudiced because of this incident."

"Yeah, that's right. I am prejudiced!" shouted Brian at the top of lungs. "And I don't want to see this freaky bird around me anymore, or I'll kill it."

Rufus growled, and then something happened that Holly had never seen before: Rufus shouted.

"This is not acceptable, Brian! If you can't keep your emotions under control that is your problem, but do not let it out on an innocent bird." He turned around and stormed off.

"Stupid idiot," Brian shouted after him and stomped back

up to his room.

"I'm sorry," Holly said to Villa Nonesuch as tears welled up in her eyes. "If you need some help, let me know."

"Thank you, my dear," the tree house said, sobbing.

Holly went back to her room feeling sad and angry. Ever since she had returned to Magora, she had been useless. She hadn't been able to help Villa Nonesuch's seedlings—and she hadn't been able to save Ileana either.

The weather seemed to echo Holly's mood. All weekend long it rained. She stared out of the living room window, trying to think of a plan to find the Golden Maple Tree. Rufus hadn't come out of his room since the fight with Brian, and Brian didn't speak a word to anyone. Villa Nonesuch wept non-stop, while Cookie kept to himself, working secretly on something in one of the barns. Amanda used her time to mix up anti-wrinkle masks and talcum powder.

Sunday evening around ten, Rufus' door flung open. He went down into the living room. The moment Brian saw him he looked the other way. Rufus responded by turning his back to Brian and facing Holly.

"We have a quite extensive schedule," said Rufus, pulling out a paper from his pocket. "We have two new classes on Monday: Color Painting I and Aqua-inking. I suggest you go to bed so you will not oversleep again tomorrow."

"What is Aqua-inking?" asked Amanda from the kitchen, her hands covered in white goop with pieces of cucumber stuck in it.

"It is a sport," said Rufus, frowning. "It takes place in a pool of different colored inks. It is rather unsophisticated, but

it is very popular here in Magora. I do not look forward to participating in this Paleolithic pastime."

"'Paleo-what?" Amanda asked.

"The Paleolithic period was a time during the Stone Age when—"

"Yeah, yeah, yeah," interrupted Holly, knowing that Rufus was about to give a speech. "We get it: Aqua-inking is old."

"They say the sport has its origin in ancient times," explained Rufus. "It is said to have a religious background and that it was first played by monks."

"At what time are we going to have that class tomorrow?" Amanda asked.

"Haven't you looked at your schedule?" Brian asked.

"I'm way too busy developing an anti-wrinkle cream," said Amanda, pouring greenish syrup into the white cucumber goop.

"The class starts—" Holly was interrupted in the middle of her sentence by a hammering on the door. "Who's there?" she asked.

"It's me, Calvin."

"Come in," Holly said. "The door is open."

Ileana's brother entered the tree house.

"Ileana is getting worse," said Calvin. "You can barely see her head anymore. The holes have spread all over her forehead and nose. We need more blood to stabilize her."

"But what can I do?" Holly asked. "My blood doesn't help her much."

"It helps her a little," said Calvin. "The nurses aren't giving her any blood at all anymore. They say it's a waste because the blood can be used for others who will recover. Your blood might stabilize her for at least a few days."

"Should I come now?" Holly asked.

"Professor Kaplin has injected her with a serum, and she is asleep now. It's probably better if you come early tomorrow."

"I will," said Holly. "But we have to find a permanent solution. I think the leaves of the Golden Maple Tree might just do that."

Her friends nodded.

"Tomorrow morning then," said Calvin, and he closed the door behind him.

The next morning, Holly got up an hour early. She prepared breakfast for the others because Villa Nonesuch was still in no state to do anything but weep. Holly saddled up Whitespot and headed for the infirmary.

When she stepped into Ileana's room, she barely recognized her. All that was left of her was a few pieces of flesh connected through pencil lines that hovered in the air. The two holes that resembled her eyes were still intact, but her nose and forehead had vanished.

Holly felt like shouting out loud in frustration, but she knew this would have not helped Ileana. What she needed now was help.

"Quick, let's give her some blood," Holly said.

Kaplin connected the tubes, and while Holly felt her blood leaving her body, she stared at Ileana, hoping that it would have a positive effect on her right away. But besides a few inches of skin appearing on her cheeks nothing happened. Holly wondered if it was really worth the effort, but the professor assured her that it kept her stable, even if it did not improve her condition.

After the transfusion, Kaplin asked, "Could you come back once a week? This might help us keep her stable a bit longer."

"Of course," said Holly, sighing as she left the infirmary.

Head drooping, she walked to the classrooms.

"Did you donate enough blood?" echoed a shrill voice behind her.

Holly turned around. Ms. Hubbleworth was standing in front of her.

"I was worried about Ileana," said the professor. "I had to check on her. If I were you Holly, I would come daily and donate blood."

"But Professor Kaplin said once a week," Holly said.

"Professor Kaplin just doesn't want you to weaken too much, but if Ileana were my friend, I wouldn't mind being a little weak. I wouldn't want to see her dissolve completely."

Holly nodded, though she wondered if the memory of her nosy neighbor had come back. "Professor, do you remember Donkleywood now?"

Ms. Hubbleworth blinked nervously as if a bug were stuck in her eye.

"The police are looking for you in Donkleywood," Holly continued. "You disappeared and they don't know you're here. You have to go back."

"I don't know what you are talking about," said Ms. Hubbleworth. "Donate blood, and don't spend too much time thinking."

As she walked away, the nasty macaw appeared between

the limestone gargoyles on top of the pillars that supported the vaulted ceiling. Squawking, it pounced on Ms. Hubbleworth's huge sunhat. The decorations on the hat swayed back and forth dangerously when the macaw shot back up.

A moment later, it dropped very low and shot parallel to the ground at Ms. Hubbleworth. "Get away from me," she shouted. The macaw buried his beak deep into her ankle. She screamed.

Holly watched the scene in disbelief. Hadn't Ms. Hubbleworth and the nasty parrot gotten along well from the first day they met? What had happened? Never before had she seen the bird behave this way toward Ms. Hubbleworth. Something was not right, but Holly couldn't figure out what it was.

Color Painting

Objects can look very real in paintings. But does looking real make them real?

Ms. Hubbleworth smashed the macaw against one of the limestone pillars. It slid down to the ground, flapped its wings twice, and fluttered back up to the gargoyles. There it remained, squawking at her as she staggered out of the corridor, and disappeared down a staircase.

Holly ran after her. The macaw swooped down and whizzed an inch over Holly's head. At that precise moment, she heard Cuspidor's voice calling her name once again. She pressed her hands against her temples and continued running. Just as the macaw was only feet away from her, Holly reached the staircase. She hopped down a few steps and slammed the door shut. A muffled bang on the other side indicated that the bird had just crashed into the door.

"That was close," Holly said to herself.

The bell rang through the corridors.

Still irritated by what had just happened, Holly pulled the schedule out of her pocket and read, "Color Painting I in Multi-hued Classroom." She was going to be late if she didn't hurry up.

Holly sped along one of the many corridors of Cliffony. As she reached the classroom, she found Brian, Rufus, and Amanda in front of it.

"It's about time," Rufus said.

He pushed the door to the Multi-hued classroom open and entered.

Holly, Brian, and Amanda trailed after him.

Paintbrushes were attached to the walls of the classroom. Their tips flickered like torches. A slender lady in her thirties with white-blonde hair that reached all the way down to her knees stood in front of them. Her pale skin turned even whiter when she noticed Rufus.

"Ethan?" she said and put her hands over her mouth. Her panic seemed to grow as she saw Holly and Brian. "Y-y-you too?" she stuttered behind her hands.

Amanda squeezed herself between Holly and Brian. At that precise moment, the lady dropped both her hands and let out a terrifying scream. Then she fainted and fell forward onto her desk. Holly rushed over, but the lady had already recovered consciousness.

She gaped at Amanda as she stuttered, "S-s-sometimes things don't have explanations. You have to take them as they are." She picked up the train of her white silken dress and draped it over her arm as she tried to compose herself. "So let's continue and never mind the brief interruption. I faint easily for no reason whatsoever. Nothing to worry about."

Holly did not understand what had just happened. The professor's reaction seemed so odd—and it was clear that they, especially Amanda, had caused it.

The lady straightened herself up. "Welcome everybody to Color Painting I," she announced. "My name is Cynthia Kasmera. I will be your instructor for the next three years. Would you please take a seat?"

A squeak sounded from Holly's backpack as she sat down. Tenshi was bouncing up and down inside. She opened it and Tenshi jumped out, pointing frantically at Professor Kasmera.

"Quiet." Holly grabbed him by the ears, and pushed him back inside.

But Tenshi did not quiet down. It seemed that Kasmera had really excited him.

"I won't be bringing him to this class anymore," Holly whispered to Brian. "He never made such a fuss before."

Professor Kasmera wiped the blackboard with her long, slender fingers and wrote down her name. Then she asked the students to write their names on slips of paper and place them on their desks so she would learn who they all were.

"Since color painting is a very difficult subject, I will need a few assistants to help me," she said.

Two hands shot up in the front row.

Holly frowned. "Did you know Gina would be in our class?" she asked Brian.

Brian shook his head. "Not only her. Look who's with her."

Holly stretched to see who the other person who had raised his hand was. It was Eric Lismahoon. He was somewhat of a personal bodyguard to Gina. Holly had encountered him a few times last year.

"We would like to volunteer to be your assistants," Lismahoon said.

"What an idiot," said Brian. "He might as well lick Gina's boots."

A gentle smile stole over Professor Kasmera's pale face. "I'm sorry, but I have picked my assistants already."

Gina's hand instantly dropped, and her face turned as purple as her sweater.

Kasmera brushed her hair over her right shoulder and sat down behind her desk. She clapped her hands twice, and a dozen lights swooped down from the ceiling. They flew through the room at rapid speed, swung around the paintbrushes on the walls, and landed gently on her desk. Only then did Holly notice these were not ordinary lights.

"Please welcome my assistants," the professor said.

The creatures lined up on the desk, facing the class while leaving a space in the middle where Kasmera leaned forward. "These are my Sylkies. Come closer if you like." The professor waved the students over.

Everybody moved in to get a closer look at these odd creatures. Holly climbed up on one of the chairs to look over the crowd that had gathered. Brian and Rufus climbed up next to Holly.

The Sylkies were hovering a few inches over the professor's desk. They looked like miniature copies of Kasmera. The major difference, besides being just about five inches tall, was their skin. They were transparent. Rainbows shimmered in the glassy skin of each one.

"Jeepers," said Holly. "Look at them." She nudged Rufus in his side.

"Sylkies are said to be the oldest creatures in Magora," said Rufus. "If you did not know about them, you would not notice them, because when they fly they look like fireflies."

Kasmera clapped her hands, and one of the Sylkies shot back up to the ceiling. The others trailed after her.

They circled above their heads. Their thin bodies had turned into nothing but lights. One of the lights increased its speed and the others followed. Holly held her breath as they spun around faster and faster, until no individual light was visible anymore. All that remained was a bright lamp on the ceiling.

"Jeepers, they can change shapes," Holly said in surprise.

Kasmera gave a brief chortle. "They are not shape-shifters. They are living lamps."

Holly got off the chair and pushed her way through the crowd to the professor so she could see her better.

"Every light you see here in Magora is composed of a group of Sylkies," Kasmera explained. "They come in all kinds of disguises." She pointed at the paintbrushes at the walls. "Sylkies hover on each tip, creating the light we see."

Kasmera clapped her hands a few times and said, "Please, everybody sit down again."

Holly frowned at Rufus as she sat down. "You knew all

that, didn't you? Why didn't you tell me?"

"Magora has many wonders, and if I tried to explain them all to you, I would be busy for the next twenty years," said Rufus. "Besides, if you did a little bit more reading you would have found out yourself. Did you never wonder what those lights were when we slid through the tunnel to get to Magora?"

"You mean, those lights are Sylkies, too?" asked Holly, remembering when they had entered the painting of Magora in the barn.

"Of course they are," said Rufus. "You heard what she said, all lights are Sylkies, also the lights on the carriages."

"And I thought they were fireflies," said Holly, dazzled from all the news she had just discovered. "But what are—"

A loud bang interrupted Holly. On his way back to his seat, Brian had fallen face first on the ground. Gina was standing behind him, grinning.

Brian jumped up and ran toward Gina. "You trip me up again and I'll—"

At the same moment, Lismahoon leaped in front of Gina, protecting her from Brian's attack. Just as Brian and Lismahoon were about to jump at each other's throats, Kasmera clapped her hands twice. The lamp above dissolved into separate lights, and in a split second, the Sylkies dropped in between the two boys and formed a glass wall. The boys slammed into it. Both screamed and held their bleeding noses.

"I'm sorry about this," said the professor. "Sylkies are very helpful when it comes to controlling aggression."

One of the Sylkies fluttered to Kasmera, landed on her shoulder, and whispered something in her ear.

"I didn't start it," said Brian. "She tripped me first." He pointed at Gina.

"Baloney," said Gina. "You tripped over your own feet."

Professor Kasmera brushed her hair to one side and nodded to the Sylkie. "Ms. Chillingham, you will have detention this weekend for inappropriate behavior."

"But I didn't do anything," Gina complained.

"Lying is a vice you should learn to abandon," said Kasmera. "The Sylkies saw what really happened."

"So now we are being watched like prisoners," muttered Gina as she plunged back onto her seat.

Brian rubbed his nose. "It hurts," he said. "Stupid wall."

"And you should learn how to control yourself, Andrew," Kasmera said.

"My name is not Andrew," Brian said.

The professor looked slightly confused for a moment, and then said, "Well, of course." She hesitated for a second. "Brian, correct?"

He nodded.

She picked up a book from her desk and dropped it onto Brian's desk. It read, *Controlling Aggression*.

"Your assignment will be to copy this book. Now let's get back to work." She clapped her hands again.

The Sylkies shot up to the ceiling and flew back and forth like balls at a Ping-Pong match. After the fifth pass, the ceiling started to glow. Another two passes and it seemed as if the limestone began to dissolve.

"What is happening?" asked Holly. She couldn't really make out clear lines anymore. It was as if she were looking at the ceiling with a pair of unfocused binoculars. Everything seemed blurry for a moment until the lines sharpened again. The limestone ceiling was no longer. Hundreds of cubes of all sizes made up the ceiling above them. They were illuminated from within, like Chinese lanterns.

One of the Sylkies maneuvered between the cubes until it reached a shiny red one. It pulled it out, fluttered above Holly's desk, and dropped it. The cube fell like a stone toward Holly. Instinctively, she fell to her knees and swung herself out of its path into the aisle. She banged her head on the bench.

The whole class laughed as the cube abruptly stopped half a foot above Holly's desk and calmly hovered in the air.

"What are you laughing about?" said Holly, frowning. "How should I have known that this thing would stop before it hit me?"

Gina jumped up from her bench. "You are a Gindar, aren't you? Gindars should know such things." She grinned. "Or maybe you're not a Gindar after all."

Holly rubbed her head as she got back up on her feet. "Shut up, Gina. I'm sick and tired of you. You're just jealous that you aren't a Gindar."

Gina hissed at her and her snake eyes turned into slits. "What should I be jealous about? Maybe about not having any parents, like you?"

"Enough," Kasmera said. "No more fighting in my class."

Holly clenched her fists but sat back down.

At that moment, more cubes began dropping down from the ceiling. Each one stopped in the air and hovered above the students' desks.

"We will now begin with our first lesson," said Kasmera. "The cubes in front of you are your color wheels. You will find out they can be wheels in a moment. They will be of utmost importance to this class. They contain all the colors that exist in the world. You will need to select the colors you want and apply them to your creation."

Professor Kasmera walked down the aisle and stopped in front of Holly. "Ms. O'Flanigan, would you please touch the cube with your paintbrush?"

Holly did what the professor asked. The cube spun around and unfolded to a flat surface. The flat surface started spinning around in a circle, as if someone had stuck a pin in the center of it. It started sending out rays of light in all directions. The outlines of the surface became blurred as it spun faster and faster until the shape turned into a wheel. At the height of its speed, it stopped abruptly. The unfolded cube was gone. A color wheel, as big as a frying pan, hovered in the air. It displayed all kinds of colors ranging from yellow and magenta to turquoise and indigo.

A delighted laugh came from the bench behind Holly. Amanda jumped up and stared excitedly at the color wheel. "Isn't it gorgeous?"

"I bet in her mind she's already using the colors for lipstick," said Brian. He leaned back on the bench, crossing his arms behind his head. "This is a waste of time. Black and white is much cooler."

"Would you please select a color and touch it again?" said Professor Kasmera, ignoring Brian's comment.

Holly wiped her brush over the red swatch on the top. The

wheel spun like a merry-go-round, and the colors changed into sections of red. Each one had a number that floated next to the color around the wheel.

Professor Kasmera nodded, and Holly touched a dark red swatch with the number 1287. The wheel spun around again, and many different variations of dark red appeared.

"Is this ever going to end?" complained Brian, yawning. "I think the shape of an object is more important than its color."

Holly touched another swatch. Again, the wheel turned, but this time it settled in a new form. Twelve dark red patches formed a perfect rectangle, leaving about two inches of space in between each swatch. Each patch had a number of up to eleven digits underneath. The reds in front of Holly looked the same.

"What now?" asked Holly. "They all look the same to me."

Professor Kasmera glided back to her desk in front of the class. "And here we learn our first lesson. Colors might appear the same at first sight, but once you train the eye you will see major distinctions." She leaned against the desk. "Can anyone see a difference between these twelve swatches?"

A murmur went through the class as everybody stared at the colors that seemed identical.

"Anyone?" Professor Kasmera asked again.

Silence hung over the classroom until Amanda blared out, "It's so obvious."

Holly turned back to Amanda and asked, "What is obvious?"

"The color on the top right is much brighter than the one next to it, and the one below doesn't have as much intensity."

The students stared at Amanda with astonished expressions on their faces.

"You have good eyes, Ms. Heavenlock. I wouldn't have expected anything less from you," Kasmera said.

Holly wondered how Kasmera could have known that Amanda had good eyes, but she didn't say anything. Instead, she looked closely at the colors. "There's no difference," Holly said, almost poking her eye on the corner of the color swatches. "There isn't one that is brighter."

Amanda got up from her bench and walked over to Holly's desk. "I wouldn't pick these three reds," she said, pointing at the bottom row. "These colors are almost as nasty as the color of her sweater." Amanda gestured at Gina. "These have blue mixed in. But this here," she pointed at the center swatch, "is the perfect color for nail polish. Intense and dark, but still alive."

Brian rolled his eyes as he pushed his glasses up on his nose. "She's making it up," he said, as he examined the reds. "I don't see any blue."

"I hate to disappoint you, Mr. Findley," said Professor Kasmera, "but there is a difference. Would you please touch each of the two swatches twice?"

Brian touched one of the swatches. As if he had won in a game show, the swatch lit up and the lights in the classroom flickered. Nervously everybody looked up at the ceiling.

Projectile Brushstrokes II

Objects might seem real when described in books. But would they be considered real even though they physically don't exist, except in our minds?

The cubes on one half of the ceiling changed to dark red. The color spread down the walls, onto the floor, and covered each chair, desk, and lamp on the left side of the classroom.

Brian touched the second swatch with his brush. Once again, the lights flickered, and another red appeared on the other half of the ceiling. It spread down the walls, dividing the room into a dark and a lighter crimson.

"These reds are completely different," Brian said,

astonished.

Professor Kasmera stepped onto the line where the two colors met. "You are very right, Mr. Findley." Kasmera swung her paintbrush, and the classroom changed back to its original color. "When you look at the colors on a larger scale, it's easier to spot the difference."

Brian nodded while the professor handed out a stack of parchment to each student.

Holly flipped through the pages. Not a single sentence was written on them. Each parchment was filled with a list of many numbers, each one with a color swatch behind it.

"Memorize these numbers and the colors that go with them. It's due next week."

Holly gulped and raised her hand as a grumble went through the class.

"Yes?" Kasmera said.

"Why do we have to memorize all these numbers?" asked Holly. "We can always take out the color wheel and just go through it until we find what we want, can't we?"

"You could do that if you had lots of time," explained Professor Kasmera. "But usually you don't. When you want to create something, you have to say the number and make the brushstroke in the air."

"But there are millions of colors," Holly said.

"And there are millions of numbers," replied Professor Kasmera. "This is the challenge of color painting and why every painter uses a different palette."

"Bummer," said Holly. "It's all about memorization. But why don't we ever hear adults saying numbers out loud when creating something?"

"After you have learned how to apply the color by saying the number, you will learn to apply it by only thinking about it," explained Professor Kasmera. "But that is advanced color painting."

After memorizing for a while a few color numbers, the bell rang.

"That's it for today. Don't forget your homework." Professor Kasmera opened the classroom door.

Holly rolled up the parchment and dropped it into her backpack. "Great. I was never good with numbers."

"I knew this class would suck," Brian said.

"I think it's a great class," said Amanda, closing her color wheel with the tip of her paintbrush.

"Easy for you to say," said Holly as they headed out the door. "You can see the difference between the colors. You don't need to remember all these numbers."

"I'm sure you'll learn them," Amanda said.

Holly and her friends left the classroom.

As they strolled down the corridor, Brian said, "Wasn't that strange how Professor Kasmera called Rufus 'Ethan' and me 'Andrew'?"

"And then she fainted when she saw me," Amanda added.

"Yes, that was strange," said Holly. "I wonder what she's hiding."

"She is just another crazy professor," said Rufus. "I have something much more interesting to tell you all."

Holly glanced at him. "What?"

"I found out something about Cuspidor. I got a special

pass from Professor LePawnee to do research in the Momarian Hell Library, and you won't believe what I found."

"You went back to the Momarian Hell Library?" Holly asked. "Why didn't you tell us?"

"I wanted to wait until I had found something," Rufus said. "There are books about Magora that haven't been touched in centuries."

"What did you find out?" Holly asked.

Rufus opened his bag and was about to pull out a book when Professor Hubbleworth approached them.

"Hello children," said the professor. "How are you doing today?"

"Thank you, we're fine," said Holly. "By the way, I thought about your suggestion, and I think you're very right: I should donate blood more than once a week."

A disapproving expression crept over Ms. Hubbleworth's wrinkly face. "More than once a week?" she repeated, surprised.

"Yes," Holly said.

"More than once a week is way too dangerous for your health," said the professor. "You shouldn't do that."

"But you suggested it yourself," Holly said.

"I would never suggest such a dangerous thing." Ms. Hubbleworth threw her head back indignantly and walked off.

"She said the opposite just a few hours ago," said Holly, confused.

"I guess the effect of the Mind-Splitting Powder is not wearing off," Amanda said.

The bell echoed again.

"But I—" said Rufus, still holding the book in his hand.

"Later," said Holly. "I don't want to be late again. Professor Gobeli is waiting for us."

They ran through the hallways and up the Tower of Bats until they reached the classroom on the top floor.

Professor Gobeli was standing behind a desk. On top was a cage with a mouse. A tiny window behind the professor let in enough light so that they could find their way to an empty bench without falling over the other students. They sat down.

"Now that we are all here, let's start the advanced class of Projectile Brushstrokes," Gobeli said as she turned around. "It's a bit stuffy in here, isn't it?"

The professor opened the window, and a breeze swept into the tower.

Holly remembered the fun she'd had last year during this class. She had handled it without much studying and had learned the Cannon Brushstroke. At the end of school last year, that brushstroke had saved her from Cuspidor and from drowning in the waters of Lake Santima.

Holly was just wondering what she would learn this year when a familiar squawking echoed through the tower.

Gobeli flung her hands up into the air and yelled, "Everybody out of here."

A swarm of Chandrills shot through the open window. The professor leaped forward, but the swarm threw her back against the desk.

"Let's go," Holly shouted, pointing at the spiral staircase.

Professor Gobeli clapped her hands once. Holly heard a

rustle above. She looked up. Hundreds of bats hung in the dusty rafters. They opened their wings and plummeted down as the students began to scream.

The Redirection
Brushstroke

If you painted a painting in a painting, would that second painting be real? It is still a painting, even though it is in another painting.

The classroom became a battleground. Hundreds of leaves sailed down on the students as the bats chopped up the Chandrills.

"Get off me!" screamed Holly, pulling one of them from her knitted cap as she stumbled toward the spiral staircase.

Professor Gobeli reached the window. She slammed it shut and stopped the flow of Chandrills entering the room. The remaining ones fluttered around a few more seconds. Then the bats turned them into piles of leaves.

"Everything is okay," said Professor Gobeli.

She clapped her hands. The bats swooped back up to the ceiling and nestled calmly in the rafters as if nothing had happened.

"I'm sorry for the interruption," said Gobeli. She picked up a dead bat, which had been killed during the attack. Gobeli had a sad look on her face. "These Chandrills are getting more aggressive every day. We've met about it, but we haven't figured out what to do."

The class piled up the leaves against the walls of the room and reassembled the benches that had been knocked over. Professor Gobeli ignited a few torches.

"If nothing is done, Gobeli won't have any bats left," Holly said to Amanda as she flicked another dead bat into the pile of leaves.

"Why haven't the professors found something to get rid of the Chandrills?" Amanda asked.

"We have tried to kill them off with poison," said Gobeli. "But it doesn't seem to work. We keep looking to find something that will work against them, but it seems the Chandrills don't react to anything. So far the only thing that can destroy them is bats."

"We really need to find the Golden Maple Tree," said Amanda. "What did you find out at the Momarian Hell Library?" She turned to Rufus. "Was there anything interesting?"

"I have checked the library from top to bottom," said Rufus. "The Golden Maple Tree does not seem to exist."

Holly was curious about what Rufus had found, but just as she was about to ask him, the professor clapped her hands.

"Let's get back to business," said Gobeli. She picked up the cage with the mouse. "Today we will start with the Redirection Brushstroke." She clapped her hands again. A few bats carried a wooden box down from the rafters and dropped it on the floor in front of the professor. A piece of cheese had been placed in one of its corners.

"This mouse hasn't eaten anything in three days," said Gobeli, "so she will head right for the cheese." She placed the cage in the box.

"Let me show how the Redirection Brushstroke works." Gobeli opened the cage, and sure enough, the mouse headed straight toward the cheese. The professor pointed her paintbrush at the mouse. A stream of white paint shot out and hit the mouse on its back. It halted abruptly, took a 90-degree turn, and ran drowsily in another direction. Then it stopped.

"Now is the moment that the mind is overcoming the reflex of the body that was caused by the brushstroke," explained Gobeli. "The mouse will realize that it's not going the right way." It poked its nose in all directions and ran back toward the cheese.

The professor flicked the brush again, and the mouse made another 90-degree turn.

"Nobody can escape the Redirection Brushstroke," she said. "All you can do is minimize the recovery time. Some people are better than others. Animals usually need about twenty seconds to recover, but human response time can vary between two and ten seconds. It takes a lot of practice to focus your mind so that you won't lose control for too long. The more you work on this, the better you get at applying the brushstroke and resisting it."

Holly was wondering how effective that brushstroke would be on Cuspidor. Could she use it in case she had to face him again?

"Are we in any danger?" asked a girl from the back of the room.

Professor Gobeli grinned. "Wasn't the Chandrill attack enough danger for you? Next time, try the brushstroke on one of them."

The girl nodded.

The professor clapped her hands again. The bats dropped down from the ceiling and hovered above the class like a black blanket. "Would you please clear your seats? We will now practice this brushstroke in groups."

The students lined up against the walls, while the bats swooped underneath the benches and tables, lifted them up, and carried them to the ceiling, where they stored them in the rafters.

"Much better," said Gobeli. "Now we have some space."

Gobeli paired the students off and explained how the brush had to be flicked.

A few moments later, Holly practiced the Redirection Brushstroke on Rufus. At first, it was difficult to control Rufus, but after the fourth trial he turned every five seconds. Rufus was able to do the same thing with Holly after a few tries, but neither Brian nor Amanda seemed to know what they were doing. Both were flicking their brushes in all directions, but neither of them could make it work.

Gina, however, seemed capable of manipulating Lismahoon

so much that he even ran straight into the wall and repeated this three more times until he fell over backward. Other students were less successful in achieving what they were supposed to do. Although they tried to make their partners turn, some ended up making them spin in circles, jump up and down, or slap themselves in the face instead.

Holly was about to swing her brush at Rufus again when Brian knocked her over, walking like a zombie toward the spiral staircase without looking back at her. Amanda followed him in the same manner. She would have stepped on Holly if Holly hadn't rolled out of her path.

For a moment, Holly was irritated, but then she realized they were both under the Redirection Brushstroke. She jumped back up on her feet and looked around to see who was responsible for her friends' abnormal behavior.

Gina stood with her back against the wall, grinning. She pointed at Holly and flicked her paintbrush.

Holly leaped into a pile of leaves, escaping the thread of white paint from Gina's brush. She scrambled back up onto her feet and shot a thread of paint back, hitting Gina with the Redirection Brushstroke. Instantly, Gina took a 90-degree turn and ran full speed against the wall.

Brian and Amanda had regained control of themselves, and they applauded.

Gina touched the bruise on her forehead that was the result of running into the wall and furiously turned to Holly. "You are going to regret that."

Holly pointed her paintbrush at Gina, ready to protect herself against whatever Gina had planned.

"Everybody, please stop now," said Professor Gobeli. "I want you to practice this brushstroke at home." She clapped her hands, and the bats carried down the benches and tables from the rafters. "Before you take off for your next class, I want to introduce another brushstroke."

Holly's fist dropped to her side. "This time you're lucky, snake," she said to Gina as the bell began to ring.

They left the Tower of Bats.

"Let's go and have lunch before Aqua-inking," Rufus said.

The four entered the cafeteria next to the Grand Hall. A mixture of delicious smells from tomato soup to freshly-baked bread filled the room. A corridor with arches on both sides led to the lunch hall. Underneath the arches, tables had been set up. Dozens of baskets filled with bread, fruits, and sweets had been placed on the tables. In the back, cauldrons steamed over open fires. All the baskets, cauldrons, and other containers had legs and arms. They walked in between the tables, handing the students the food they had ordered.

"I think I'll have some carrot cake with chocolate syrup today," Brian said.

"You should eat something healthy for a change," Rufus said, picking up a bright pink vegetable shaped like a cross between a cucumber and a star fruit.

Brian threw back his head, laughing. "Your healthy diet is really paying off," he said. "You're still the shortest of us all."

Rufus glanced briefly at his reflection in a shiny cauldron. "Height is not a reflection of healthy living," he said and turned away.

Holly filled up her plate and headed to the hall. Sunlight

fell through the giant stained-glass windows and brightened up the room like a kaleidoscope. Hundreds of students occupied the round tables in the hall.

"Holly, come sit here," a boy shouted across a few tables.

It was Marvin, giving her that familiar smile, pointing at an empty seat beside him.

Holly felt as if a sudden heat wave engulfed her. Embarrassed, she turned away.

"Come over here," said Amanda, who had managed to secure a table for them.

Holly sat down between Amanda and Rufus.

"I still have not told you what I found out," Rufus said.

Holly remembered that Rufus had been trying to tell them something, but Ms. Hubbleworth had gotten in the way. She was curious to find out if Rufus might have found a way to help Ileana. But instead, Rufus pulled out a book from his bag.

"Cuspidor has a daughter," he said.

Unexpected News

Can something that exists in a fiction book be real? I believe it can. It is real in your mind, and the mind defines what is real and what is not.

Holly jumped up from the table, her chair falling backward with a thump. The students at the tables around them turned their heads.

"A daughter?" she asked.

Holly stood rooted to the spot. She could not believe that this monster had a child. Realizing what attention she had aroused, she picked up her chair and sat back down. The students around them resumed their conversation.

"It is not one hundred percent sure," said Rufus. "There is only one brief note about her in the book."

"Is she alive?" Holly asked.

"The book does not say," Rufus said.

Holly's stomach turned. She felt like throwing up. There was only one other Gindar in Magora other than Cuspidor— her.

"Do you think I-I-I could be his daughter?" Holly stammered. "I mean, he's a Gindar and I am, too. And I can hear him in my head."

"I know you miss having parents," said Brian, "but you can't be so desperate that you want Cuspidor to be your father."

"Both of you are being ridiculous," said Rufus. "It is ludicrous to think Holly could be Cuspidor's daughter. He is a painting, and you are a real person."

"It's not that I want him as a father, but if it's true, I have to find out," Holly said. She got up from the table. "I'm going to ask Professor LePawnee. If I'm not Cuspidor's daughter, I might at least find out who this daughter might be." Holly pushed her plate at Brian. "Here, you can have my chocolate cake."

"I'm done," said Amanda, rushing after Holly. "I'm coming with you."

A few minutes later, the two girls knocked at Professor LePawnee's office. The door flew open by itself.

"Come in," said the professor.

She went to a trolley among piles of parchment stacked up all over the room. Never before had Holly seen LePawnee's office in such a mess.

"Would you like a cup?" said the professor as she picked up a teapot from the trolley.

"No, thanks," said Holly. "I've come to ask you something

very important."

"And that is?" asked Professor LePawnee. "Amanda? Tea?"

"No, thanks," said Amanda. "We found out that Cuspidor had a daughter."

LePawnee set down the teapot. "You mean that rumor?"

Holly nodded. "You've heard about that?"

"That rumor has been going around for ages, but there is no proof that it's true," said LePawnee. "There is only one book in the library that mentions a daughter, but we don't know anything else about her. So it is more a legend than a fact."

"What I'm really worried about is that I might be his daughter," Holly said.

The professor laughed. "Oh, don't you worry. It's just a myth. There is no daughter, and if there were, you certainly wouldn't be her."

"How can you be so sure?" Holly asked.

LePawnee waved her hand, and the entrance door swung open again. "I just am." With a gentle gesture to leave the room, she said, "You are late for Aqua-inking class."

"Fine," said Holly. She stepped out of the office and closed the door behind her. "That wasn't really helpful at all."

"But she seemed pretty convinced that you're not his daughter," Amanda said.

"Yes, but why?" Holly was not sure whether she could believe LePawnee or not, but she had no other choice than to accept what the professor had said.

"We'd better get to class," Amanda said.

Holly nodded.

"Aqua-inking takes place in the courtyard," said Amanda, running her index finger along the crumpled schedule in her hand.

A few minutes later, they reached the courtyard. It was raining. Holly stepped into the colonnade, sat down between the finely carved limestone columns, and looked up into the sky. Nobody was there. Only a swarm of bats circled above.

"Bummer. We missed them," Holly said. "They must have left."

"Wait a second," said Amanda. "There's Ms. Hubbleworth. Maybe she knows where the class went."

Ms. Hubbleworth was stumbling along the cloister, pursued by her macaw. She flung her arms above her sunhat, trying to protect it from the bird's attack.

"Strange," said Holly. "She doesn't seem to get along with her parrot anymore at all. They were such good friends at the beginning."

"Professor Hubbleworth," Amanda shouted along the cloister. "Can you tell us where the—"

"No time," Ms. Hubbleworth yelled back as she dashed off, chased by the macaw only feet behind her.

"That didn't help us much," said Amanda. She leaned against the column opposite Holly. "What are we going to do now?"

Silence hung in the air. Only the rustling of the wind in the bushes and the pouring rain echoed in the courtyard. The rustling reminded Holly of the bushes outside the Smoralls' mansion. Donkleywood was now so far away, and so many things had changed since they had entered Magora. Back then,

Holly felt that having Amanda around was the worst thing that had ever happened to her. She didn't feel that way anymore.

"I'm sorry, Amanda," Holly said.

"Sorry for what?"

"A year ago, I thought you were the worst jerk in the world. I really hated that you treated me as if I wasn't as cool as you." Holly's head drooped.

"Actually," said Amanda. "I was a jerk. I judged you by how you were dressed and what you drew. I should have seen that you're pretty cool."

"I didn't know what a good friend you could be," Holly said.

"Excuse me," echoed a loud voice through the courtyard. "May I interrupt your conversation?"

Amanda rummaged in her backpack and pulled out the gnarled branch. Villa Nonesuch's eye was wide open. "I have dinner prepared. Be home at 5 p.m. sharp."

"She's back," said Holly, excited. "Are you all right?"

"I'm okay. I just needed some time for myself," said Villa Nonesuch. "But what about you? Why aren't you in class?"

"We were late for Aqua-inking, and by the time we got here the class had left already."

"Oh dear," said Villa Nonesuch. "You really haven't read your schedules well, have you?"

"Of course we have," said Holly. "It says that Aqua-inking takes place in the courtyard."

"No, it doesn't," said the branch. "You missed something. It says sub-courtyard."

"Right," Amanda said. "But what's the difference?"

"The difference is that the field is below the courtyard. The entrance to the Aqua-inking sports hall is at the rear of the Tower of Bats. Now run along, dears." The eye blinked twice and closed.

Holly and Amanda ran through the pouring rain, covering their heads with their cloaks. At the back of the Tower of Bats, they found a staircase leading down to a rusty door. A sign with bold letters read, "Aqua-inking Sports Hall."

Aqua-inking

When I leave a painting unfinished, I can come back to it and finish it at some other time. It doesn't have to stay unfinished forever unless I have a reason to leave it in this state.

Holly and Amanda entered a dark corridor that led steeply down into the ground.

Amanda illuminated the tip of her brush. "Let's go," she said.

They followed the hallway, took a left turn, and climbed down a staircase.

"There's a light," said Amanda, pointing her paintbrush into the distance.

"That must be the Aqua-inking Sports Hall," Holly said.

The corridor opened up and led onto a platform high

above a swimming pool.

"Jeepers," said Holly. "You could fit a whole town into this place." She held on to the railing and leaned forward.

The pool below was divided into many squares. It looked like a chessboard, only that the squares were not black and white but each was filled with a different colored water. A number made out of glass hovered in the air about ten feet above each square.

Holly compared the numbers with the colors below and made the connection.

"That's the number for vermilion," said Holly, remembering the color wheel from Kasmera's class. "I bet those are the numbers from the color wheel."

Giant turtles with oddly-shaped shells were lined up in a row in the color squares at the edges. At the far end of the hall was a gigantic tree house.

"Jeepers. That's Villa Nonesuch's cousin, Villa Littlemore," said Holly in surprise.

Last year Holly had entered the Quadrennial Art Competition. In one of the tasks, Villa Littlemore had risen mysteriously out of the courtyard ground. Holly had always wondered how this tree could have appeared out of nowhere. Now it dawned on her that Villa Littlemore simply grew underneath the courtyard.

"Oh look, there's Brian and Rufus." Amanda pointed at a group of about twenty students standing at the edge of the pool. She waved at them.

The students looked up. Some waved back. Among them was the instructor. He was wearing a tight T-shirt that

emphasized his muscular upper body and black shorts that showed off his powerful calves.

"Professor Bundo," Amanda said, smiling.

Last year, Professor Bundo had been one of the first professors to welcome them to Magora. Ever since that time, Holly had wondered what function he had at Cliffony besides being the object of Amanda's crush.

"Come on, let's go see the others," Amanda said.

They climbed down the steep ladder that led to the pool.

"Where have you been?" asked Rufus. "We have been waiting for you for twenty minutes."

"I see you finally made it to Aqua-inking," said Bundo, frowning. "It's about time."

Amanda leaped forward and stretched out her hand. "Hello, Professor Bundo. It's a pleasure to have you as our instructor."

"Your friend is right. You are twenty minutes late for class," Bundo said, ignoring Amanda's hand and turning to Holly. "Same for you, Ms. O'Flanigan."

"I'm sorry," said Holly. "We couldn't find the classroom."

"She's always late," shouted a voice from behind. "She was late for every single class today."

Holly glanced over her shoulder, knowing precisely whom this voice belonged to. Gina was standing next to Lismahoon.

"Yes, Gina is right," said Lismahoon. "Holly is late all the time."

The professor turned back to Holly. "I don't want anybody late for class anymore. Is this clear?"

Holly and Amanda nodded silently.

"So now that we are all here, I would like to introduce you to Aqua-inking," said Bundo. "Aqua-inking is the oldest-known sport in Magora. Over a span of the next three years, you will not only learn how to physically play the game, but you will study the history of Aqua-inking as well. I have decided that we will jump right into the fun part and learn how to play first."

Bundo pulled a carrot out of his pocket and kneeled down at the edge of the pool. The largest turtle stretched its scaly head toward the carrot and snapped it out of the professor's hand.

"These are Turapids," explained Bundo. "If you take a closer look, you will notice they each have two footprints on their shell. Depending on the size of the turtle, the footprints vary in size as well."

Holly leaned over Brian's shoulder. He was kneeling next to Bundo.

"Why footprints?" Brian asked.

"Good question," said Bundo. "That is where the player's feet fit. Each player stands barefoot on the Turapids. Depending on where you want to go, you shift your weight to one side or the other. So if you want to take a left turn, you put pressure on your left foot and the Turapid will react to it. Of course, it takes a while to know exactly how much pressure a Turapid will need to make a 90-degree turn or an 80-degree turn. That is for you to find out during this year."

"It's a bit like skiing, isn't it?" Brian asked.

"The physical part is, but not the game itself," explained Bundo. "There are two teams, the gold and the silver teams."

He flung a chest open. T-shirts marked with golden and silver numbers were stacked up inside. "This half of the class will be the silver team," said the professor, separating the class down the middle with a gesture of his hand. "And this half will be the gold team." He pointed in Holly's direction. "Please try on a T-shirt."

Everybody rushed to the chest. Holly waited. She had no desire to fight for a shirt. By the time she got to the chest there was only one shirt left. "XXL" was written on the label.

"Great," she mumbled as she put it on. "This shirt is way too big for me."

"You don't need to wear it if you become a shiner," said Professor Bundo, taking the T-shirt out of Holly's hand. "That is a special player. If you want, you can be the shiner of the golden team."

"Whatever," said Holly. "It's better than wearing something that looks like a nightgown on me."

"Now let me explain the rules. The teams will be standing on their Turapids facing each other, as on a chessboard. Behind your team is the so-called lanteen." Bundo pointed at a pole at each side of the pool. Boxes were attached to them. "Your goal is to get to the opposite side, pick up the brush that is inside the box, and bring it back to your side. In the meantime, your team has to collect points. When you get twenty-five points, the box will open automatically. All you have to do is get the brush and bring it back to your side."

"That should be fun," said Brian. "Can we throw people into the water?"

"Touching is not allowed," said Bundo. "You only have

one option to stop the other team from getting to your side. One is the Redirection Brushstroke that you have learned from Professor Gobeli. You have to shout the transparent number above the square where your opponent is and make the Redirection Brushstroke. The other player will then make a 90-degree turn and he will be out of your way. But if your brushstroke hits the square too late and the player is already on the next square, you will lose a point. So don't overuse the Redirection Brushstroke unless you are precise and fast."

"This is so stupid," Rufus whispered. "You really do not have to use your brain much for this."

"This is not about the brain," said Brian. "It's a fun game." He turned to Bundo. "If we all zoom across the pool, there will be complete chaos. How will you be able to see if someone has fouled the other?"

"I have plenty of referees," said Professor Bundo. "The Turapids are monitoring every move you make and will inform me of any foul play."

Holly kneeled down, patting the scaly head of one of the Turapids. "So what do I have to do in all this?" she asked. "What does a shiner do?"

Bundo went to one of the Turapids and took his shoes and socks off. "A shiner can score extra points," he said. "Every few minutes one square will light up. If you touch it before it goes out, your team receives five points."

"That's easy to do," said Holly. "I don't have to play against anybody."

"Not really," said Bundo. "You have to play against the other shiner."

"The other team has one, too?" Holly asked.

"Of course," said Professor Bundo. "Ms. Chillingham has asked me if she can be the one for the silver team, so you will be competing against her."

Holly frowned, while Gina grinned.

The professor stepped onto one of the Turapids, placing his bare feet on the footprints on the shell. The creature swayed briefly. Bundo balanced his weight skillfully. "Watch my toes now." He wiggled all his toes and the Turapid accelerated forward. He stopped wiggling and it halted. Next, he shifted his weight to the right, and the creature took a right turn. "It's very easy. Everybody try it. Gold team stays here; silver team goes to the Turapids on other side."

Holly stepped skeptically onto the back of one of the creatures. It swayed considerably, but she was able to stay on top. Amanda and Rufus didn't budge. They watched Holly and Brian struggle to stay upright.

"I do not fancy this ridiculous sport," Rufus said in his fake British accent.

"I don't like it either," Amanda said. She carefully stepped onto one of the Turapids. It shook violently. "What a stu-u-upid idea," she screamed as she flung her hands abruptly back and forth. Then, she disappeared headfirst into a square of pink water.

A few bubbles appeared in the square, and a few seconds later, Amanda surfaced. She was spitting pink water.

Holly laughed out loud and reached down to Amanda to help her out.

"Pink looks really good on you," Brian said, grinning.

"Idiot," said Amanda. She wiped the colored ink off her face and climbed out of the pool.

"Showers are behind Villa Littlemore," shouted Bundo through a megaphone from the opposite side of the pool. Amanda stomped away, leaving a pink trail behind.

"Please everybody get on your Turapids," announced Bundo from the center of the pool. "Mr. Letterhead, that includes you."

"I am not going to expose myself to such a stupid game," Rufus muttered under his breath to Brian and Holly.

"Come on, Rufus," said Holly. "Sometimes you have to do things you don't like—and you want to pass this class, don't you?"

"I am not good at sports," Rufus said. "I will be the laughing stock of the entire school."

Professor Bundo sped through the pool and came to an abrupt halt in front of Rufus. "Is there a problem?"

Rufus was about to say something when Brian maneuvered his Turapid right between Bundo and Rufus, blocking their eye contact.

"Rufus isn't feeling well," said Brian. "He has an upset stomach." He glanced over his shoulder and winked at Rufus.

"Yes, I am feeling horrible," Rufus said.

Outraged, Holly put her hands on her hips and was about to say something. She couldn't believe that Brian was actually helping Rufus get out of this. Rufus needed to face his fears, or he would remain a scared chicken for the rest of his life.

But Brian maneuvered his Turapid toward Holly, blocking her view of Bundo. "Rufus gets sick very often," Brian said.

Before Holly could say a word, the professor turned toward Rufus. "All right, just watch the practice today, but next time you will have to join us." He directed his Turapid back into the center of the pool.

"Why did you help me?" Rufus whispered to Brian.

"We are still friends, aren't we?" Brian winked at Rufus. "Listen. I'm really sorry. I shouldn't have said Shardee was responsible for the death of the tree house seedlings."

"That is all right," said Rufus. "It was my fault. I should not have been so cold about all this." Rufus fidgeted as he avoided Brian's look. "You know, Brian, I-I-I," he stuttered, "I am not good when dealing with emotions. It is hard for me to show them, but I am trying really hard. Maybe one day I will be as expressive as you are." Rufus briefly glanced up at Brian.

"You don't want to be like me," said Brian. "You can get yourself in big trouble if you always say what you feel." Brian smiled, put a hand up in the air, and said, "Friends?"

"Sure," Rufus said, giving him a high-five with a smile.

"I'm glad you two have finally sorted out your differences," said Holly. "But I don't think you should be lying so blatantly."

"Relax," said Brian. "It was just an emergency, not really a lie."

"It's still a lie," said Holly. "Everybody has to do things from time to time that he doesn't like."

"I can do it next week," said Rufus as he walked away.

"Sure," hollered Holly after him. "Next week you'll have another excuse."

Christmas Shopping

When I leave a piece of writing unfinished, I can come back to it and finish it later. It doesn't have to stay unfinished forever unless I have a reason to leave it in this state.

In the following weeks, Holly's free time outside class was spent with extra practice in the Aqua-inking pool. She really wanted to beat Gina as a shiner.

In addition to her regular school work, Holly went once a week to the infirmary. She was still giving blood to Ileana, but all it did was slow down Ileana's decay a little. Each time Holly entered the infirmary room, she started trembling. After a while she dreaded each visit, since she could not see any improvement. She grew more and more miserable, and felt guilty for thinking that she did not want to do it anymore. Even though Holly kept researching at the school library, hoping to find a cure, she had come to the point where she didn't know what to do anymore.

Instead of letting herself be depressed, Holly tried to cheer herself up by playing more Aqua-inking. During each game, Gina tried to distract Holly by shouting nasty things about her not having any parents. Even though it hurt, Holly tried to ignore Gina's comments and focused on the sport.

Rufus had managed to get permission from Professor LePawnee to research Aqua-inking and write a paper instead of physically participating in the class. It annoyed Holly, but she had more pressing issues to deal with than making Rufus aware that he had to face his fears and deal with them.

Amanda, on the other hand, was practicing hard to impress Professor Bundo with her maneuvering skills, while Brian was excited that the silver team had a new member. In late November, a new student, Samantha Wang, had joined the team. Ever since that day, Brian's concentration skills had dropped. Each time Samantha zoomed by, he halted, smiled, and forgot about the game.

After many matches, Holly realized that Aqua-inking was not as exciting as she had hoped it would be. Losing every single game because of Brian and Amanda's lack of attention was not fun and did not cheer her up.

"I've had enough," Holly yelled after one of the matches when the class had ended.

She stomped out of the Aqua-inking Hall. Brian and Amanda followed her.

"I'm sorry," said Brian. "It was just that Samantha—"

"Samantha, Samantha," yelled Holly. "Couldn't you

concentrate for once on the game? That is the fourteenth time we've lost against Gina's team."

"Maybe next time we'll win," Amanda said.

"Not if you are just trying to impress Professor Bundo," Holly said.

Silence hung in the air for a few seconds.

Amanda's head drooped. "I'm sorry. You're right. I haven't been paying attention to the game."

"We should be trying to think of a way to find the Golden Maple Tree instead of playing Aqua-inking," Holly cried. "Ileana will die if we don't find a cure."

She plowed through snow piles in the courtyard, leaving Brian and Amanda behind.

All the anger she felt about not being able to help Ileana had come out.

When Holly returned to Villa Nonesuch, she locked herself in her room and didn't come out, except for school, breakfast, and dinner. Everyone left her alone, which she was grateful for.

Christmas was rapidly approaching, but Holly didn't have any desire to participate in shopping sprees along Papplewick Street. She preferred to join Rufus in the library, looking for information on the Golden Maple Tree.

It was not until the 22nd of December that Holly received an invitation from Cliffony:

Dear Student,
We would like to invite you to our annual Christmas Party.
Please join us for a fun-filled evening in the Grand Hall.

Sincerely,

Professor LePawnee, Headmistress of Cliffony Academy of the Arts.

P.S.: For details and dress code, see reverse side.

Holly was painfully reminded that last year she had missed the Christmas party because she had misused MSP and her mind was stuck in an oak tree.

Her classmates had been talking about the party for months and it was one of the most famous events in Cliffony. It would be nice to get a break and attend this time.

"Come on, my dear," said Villa Nonesuch. "You can't sit around all day."

"All right," said Holly. "I'll go and get some presents for the others."

"That's the spirit!" Villa Nonesuch said.

She snuck out of the tree house so that her friends would not see her, saddled up Whitespot, and flew to Papplewick Street.

Circling above, Holly saw that the street was packed with people carrying parcels with large ribbons. Long chains of lights dangled between the houses and illuminated the Christmas shoppers below. Most of them were not wearing ordinary black cloaks but bright red ones. It reminded Holly of a Santa Claus convention. Some of them had piled their parcels onto griffins that were parked in front of the decorated shops.

Holly veered toward the market square where she landed. "I'll be back in about an hour," she said, patting Whitespot on his head. "You wait here."

The smell of freshly-baked gingerbread and chocolate cookies hung in the air as Holly entered Papplewick Street. Christmas songs sounded everywhere, but Holly couldn't locate where they were coming from.

As she squeezed herself through the crowd of people, she noticed a bookstore with Santa Claus picture books and other Christmas publications in the window. Holly stopped. A Ledesma girl pointed at one of the picture books. The book suddenly flapped open, hovered toward the girl, and tilted so that she could read through the window.

"It's about time they improved their service," said the girl, smiling at Holly.

Holly smiled back and pointed at a thick leather-bound book. The book flapped open, and a second later, the pages were turning in front of her.

Just as Holly was about to step inside the store, someone from behind shot in front of her and opened the door.

"Marvin. What are you doing here?" Holly asked.

Marvin smiled, standing stiffly like a butler at the door. "I was looking for you."

"Why?" Holly asked, smiling back at him.

Marvin blushed slightly. "You know we have the Christmas party coming up, and I was wondering if you would come with me."

Holly's mouth dropped wide open. The whole school would whisper behind her back if she showed up with Marvin. But then again, she could use someone to cheer her up and Marvin would definitely be able to do that.

"Oh. Sure, why not?" Holly said.

Marvin stared at her in disbelief. "Really?"

"Sure, I'll go with you," Holly said.

"Great. I'll see you there," said Marvin, grinning at her.

Holly was excited that Marvin had asked her. She stepped over the threshold into the bookstore with a smile.

Ten minutes later, she had found a book for Rufus, called *Essentials of Hypothetical Painting Theory*.

The dwarf in the store packed the book. He wrapped it up in a red box that had thick lips on it. As soon as Holly lifted up the parcel, the lips started singing.

"Jingle books, jingle books, jingle all your books. Oh, what fun it is to buy in a bookstore on your way—"

"Hey," interrupted Holly. "Do I have to listen to this all the way home now?"

"If you don't like to listen to my smoothly rich baritone voice, I won't waste another note on you," said the parcel. It twisted its lips into a pout and fell silent.

Holly laughed and strolled up Papplewick Street until she reached the bakery. As soon as she opened the door, the dwarf owner welcomed her. "Howdy," he said.

"Merry Christmas, Chester," Holly replied.

The dwarf wobbled around the counter and took Holly by the hand.

"I'm sure you are still looking for a few Christmas presents," Chester said.

He led Holly into the back room. A life-size marzipan baby griffin was hovering in the air, and a gingerbread man the size of a child was riding on top.

"Jeepers," marveled Holly. "It's huge."

"I thought you might need a gift for Ileana," Chester said.

Holly gulped. She had actually forgotten about Ileana for a moment. She remembered how her friend used to stroll around the bakery. And now Ileana was in the infirmary and Holly had started to forget what she used to be like. That person lying under the tent was not Ileana anymore. It was an Unfinished. Holly's eyes dampened. She felt horrible that her friend was struggling for her life, and she was out shopping.

"Hello? Are you still there?" Chester interrupted Holly's thoughts. He was waving his hand in front of her face.

"Yes, sorry," said Holly. "I was just thinking about something. Ileana will love the griffin."

"You can have Cookie pick it up any time you want. It's yours," Chester said.

Holly paid the dwarf with 100 Q. The cube briefly opened up, and a Q-person in a caftan and a turban peeked out, gave Holly two thumbs up, and disappeared into the cube.

"That is way too much," said Chester, but Holly refused to take it back.

"Then let me give you something else." Chester reached into his pocket and handed her a leather pouch.

There was only one piece of chocolate in the pouch. Holly tossed it into her mouth.

"Tastes delicious," she said happily.

Chester pointed at the pouch again. There was another piece of chocolate that Holly hadn't seen. She ate the second piece. But when she looked into the pouch again, there was another piece of chocolate.

"Now I get it," said Holly. "There's always something inside no matter how much you take out."

Chester nodded. "I call it a chocolate cornucopia."

"This will be a great present for Brian," said Holly. "Thanks, Chester."

She packed up the pouch and left the bakery. On her way down Papplewick Street, she glanced at the old clock on the sidewalk. It was still early.

She entered Wrinkle Dimple Skin Care Shop and bought a set of lipsticks for Amanda. As she pulled out her pouch and picked 10 Q, the cube suddenly rattled.

"Financial advice," Holly mumbled, knowing that the Q people would probably tell her she shouldn't be spending so much money.

The tiny cube turned a few times in her palm and a latch opened on the top. A chubby woman with a bonnet and an apron tied around her balloon-like belly climbed out and hopped into Holly's palm.

"Never mind your finances," said the woman. "They are in good order. But I have something else to tell you." She waved her hand at Holly, indicating that she should come closer. Holly lifted the woman closer to her ear.

"I know where you can find the Golden Maple Tree," the Q-woman said.

21

The Christmas Painting

An unfinished work, painting or writing, can never become real unless it is finished. It would always linger between fantasy and reality.

Holly couldn't believe her ears. "You know where the Golden Maple Tree is?"

"It's in the monastery of Chenaab," the Q-woman said.

"How do you know that?" Holly asked.

"We hear everything that is going on outside," said the Q woman. "But never mind. You might want to check the Gallery of Wonders for a painting of this monastery. There are lots of gate paintings that lead to other places." The woman winked at Holly, climbed back into her cube, and slammed the latch shut.

"The Gallery of Wonders?" Holly said.

Of course there could be a gate painting into the monastery. She should have checked the gallery long before this. How stupid of her not to think of it.

Holly paid for the lipstick and was about to walk out the door when she saw a woman on the street looking inside. Holly stared at her in disbelief. Was she seeing a ghost? Her foster mother, Ms. Smorall, was checking out the display in the window.

An expression of fear stole over the woman's face. She turned around and hurried away.

"Ms. Smorall," Holly shouted and bolted out of the shop.

Now she knew that her foster mother was not a figment of her imagination. She was in Magora. But what was she doing here? There was only one logical explanation. Back in Donkleywood, Ms. Smorall must have followed her to the barn and jumped into the painting.

Holly crashed right into a girl who was about to enter the store and knocked her over.

"Thanks, Holly. You messed up my fingernails completely." It was Amanda, looking down mournfully at her broken nails.

"Sorry, but I just saw Ms. Smorall," said Holly. "She must have come through the painting. She's right there." Holly pointed in the direction where she had seen Ms. Smorall. But there was nobody there.

"Where?" Amanda asked.

"She was there just a moment ago," Holly said.

"Ms. Smorall doesn't even know Magora exists," said Amanda. "You probably just imagined it."

Holly nodded, but she knew that he had not imagined it.

"But what are you doing here anyhow?" Amanda asked. "You don't usually go to Wrinkle Dimple Skin Care Shop."

Holly didn't want to give away that she was shopping for Amanda's present and so she said, "Oh. Well, see, Marvin asked me out to the Christmas party, and I was just looking around to maybe get some eyeliner."

Amanda smiled with excitement. "Giving you a makeover is something I've always wanted to do." She grabbed Holly by the hand. "I'll make you look prettier than you can imagine. Let's go shopping."

Two hours later, Amanda had dragged Holly through every single shop. They bought an elegant dress, some makeup, shoes, and even a handbag. Not that Holly cared much for all of this, but she didn't want to offend Amanda, who truly wanted to do something nice for Holly. It was a well-intended effort to beautify Holly. After she had blamed Amanda for ruining the Aqua-inking game, she didn't want to strain their friendship even more.

A few days later, Christmas Eve arrived. Cookie had hung chains of lights and tinsel all over Villa Nonesuch and decorated every single room.

Amanda had spent all day long getting Holly's curls under control and fitting her into the new dress.

"You look absolutely fabulous," said Amanda. "I knew you could be the prettiest girl in the school."

"Oh, come on, Amanda," said Holly as she stepped in front of the golden-framed mirror standing next to her four-poster bed. For a moment, her gaze wandered around, searching for herself looking like a clown. But what she saw was quite the opposite. There really was a pretty girl in the mirror.

"That's me?" Holly's mouth dropped open. "I can't believe it."

The long, silken dress Holly was wearing gave her an elegance she had never had before. The crimson of the dress contrasted the light green of the eyeliner and her curls were not standing on end as usual but gently fell over her shoulders.

"So what do you think?" Amanda asked.

"You did a great job," said Holly. "You've really learned a lot about makeup since last year." She hesitated for a moment. "Please don't take this personally, but I still prefer wearing pants."

Amanda laughed. "Let's go now. Brian and Rufus have taken off on Whitespot, but Cookie left us Maroon to get to the party."

Ten minutes later, they had reached Cliffony. Holly staggered along the corridor. Never before had she worn anything other than completely flat shoes, and she had a hard time walking in ones with a higher heel.

The two girls flung open the double doors to the Grand Hall. It was empty. Not a single person, not even a bench, was inside. There was only a huge painting of a village that had been placed on an easel in the middle of the hall.

"Where is everybody?" asked Amanda as she closed the double doors behind her.

"I don't know. Do you think they left already?"

At that precise moment, a voice sounded in the empty hall. "Holly."

Holly turned around. There was nobody there, but the voice

still echoed from somewhere distant. She darted to the double doors and flung them open again. Nobody was outside.

"Cuspidor," said Holly. "He's calling my name."

Amanda stepped closer to the painting. "Baloney. I heard that voice, too, and it sounded awfully familiar."

The painting suddenly turned into particles of light. It looked like a lake glittering in the sunlight. Professor Farouche stepped out from behind the painting.

"It was about time you came," he growled. "You are late again. The party has already started." He gave Amanda a gentle push into the painting. "Now you, Ms. O'Flanigan." He pointed at Holly.

"Are you coming, too?" asked Holly as she approached the painting.

"I don't like Christmas," said Farouche as he pushed Holly into the lights.

Expecting she would slide down a tunnel as she had before, Holly hiked up her dress and braced herself for the journey. But nothing happened. She simply stepped through into a ballroom that was decorated like a French castle. The brightly-polished hardwood floors reflected the large paintings and stucco moldings on the ceiling. Mirrors in thick golden frames covered the walls. At the end of the ballroom was a silver-painted double door.

"That was an easy journey," Amanda said.

"Where are we?" Holly asked.

Amanda pointed at a sign above the double door. It read, "Christmas World."

"All right, let's see what Christmas World has in store for

us," Holly said.

She went to the door and pushed it open. They stood there staring at nothing but darkness.

The Gallery of Wonders

Once an unfinished piece of work is completed, reality and fantasy merge. Then, it becomes unclear where reality ends and fantasy begins.

Holly quickly realized she was standing on a platform high above a village, staring into the dark sky. A seemingly endless staircase led down to brightly-lit houses built out of gingerbread. The square in the distance had a towering Christmas tree in its center. Colored lights flickered on strings above the streets, and snowflakes danced around. Jolly Christmas songs sounded, and the smell of freshly-baked cookies filled the air.

Holly climbed down the staircase, awkwardly trying to keep balance in her heels. Amanda followed her. Halfway there, Holly noticed that the square was filled with students.

"Doesn't he look handsome?" said Amanda, pointing at a

boy sitting at a decorated table next to the Christmas tree.

Holly smiled. Marvin looked gorgeous in his perfectly-fitted tuxedo.

"Strange," Amanda said. "It isn't cold at all, even though it's snowing."

Holly caught a snowflake. It didn't melt in her hand.

"It's fake snow," Holly said.

"That's why it's so warm," Amanda said.

The moment the two girls were twenty stairs away from the square, a gong echoed and a sleigh with reindeer zoomed above them. Using fog, it wrote in the sky: "Welcome." The students stared up at them.

Holly felt heat rushing into her head and she knew she was blushing. How embarrassing to have half of Cliffony look at her, especially now that she was swaying in these shoes like a palm tree in a hurricane. But this was the downside of being known all over Magora.

Under the gaze of half the crowd, Holly carefully stepped down the staircase. Some boys started to whisper; others stood there with their mouths wide open.

"Why do they all have to stare at us?" Holly asked. "Is something wrong?"

"Nothing is wrong," replied Amanda. "It's just that nobody has ever seen you like this."

For the first time, Holly was getting the same amount of attention Amanda always got for her looks. Holly felt glamorous. But was this something she really wanted? No, she was not a beauty queen. She liked worn pants and baggy sweaters.

Holly glanced at Marvin. He was the only one who didn't

seem to notice her princess-like appearance. Nervously, he looked around the crowd, occasionally asking a student something.

"Please, come and sit down." A dwarf in an elf outfit welcomed Holly and Amanda. He guided them to a table decorated with a miniature Christmas tree in the middle and lots of bowls filled with cookies and sweets.

As they passed Marvin, Holly briefly smiled at him and expected him to get up and say hello. But instead of returning the smile, Marvin turned around.

"How rude was that?" said Amanda. "I can't believe he just ignored you."

"I can't blame him," said Holly. "I was supposed to meet him before the party, but I totally forgot because of the makeover. And I have ignored him a few times in the past."

At that precise moment, a loud voice said, "Holy smokes. Is that you, Holly? Wow."

Holly turned sideways. Brian was approaching, carrying a plate piled high with chocolate fudge cake. Rufus followed.

"Wow. You just look fantastic," said Brian. "I wouldn't have recognized you if Amanda hadn't been standing next to you."

"You do look rather good," Rufus said.

"Thanks, guys," said Holly, slightly embarrassed. "Do you know where I can get something to drink?"

Brian whistled, and a brush the size of an adult slid on its bristles toward them. A Santa Claus hat had been placed on its top. Two wooden arms extended from the handle to carry a tray with dozens of glasses.

"Isn't that cool?" Brian asked, laughing.

Holly grabbed a glass with a blue fruit floating on top. Brian and Rufus put their plates on the table.

"Listen, you guys," Holly said. "I have to tell you something very important."

Everybody moved a bit closer to her. Holly began telling them what she had learned about the Golden Maple Tree from the Q-person. When she was finished, there was a long silence.

Then, Brian gave his usual, "Wow."

"Do you think that is true? That the tree is in the monastery?" Rufus asked. "Why believe a Q-person about something that does not have to do with money?"

"Q-people hear a lot of secrets in their cubes," Holly said.

"Do you think there could be a painting that leads us directly to the monastery?" Amanda asked.

"We have to search the gallery as soon as we can," Holly said.

"We can do that tomorrow morning," Rufus said.

"I guess it is already morning," said Holly. "The sun is coming up." She pointed at a bright sphere up in the sky.

Rufus laughed. "That is not the sun. This is one of the magic balloons. They float in the air like suns, but they are for decoration purposes only."

Rufus climbed on a chair and tried to reach the balloon that flickered like a yellow sun. At that precise moment, Marvin passed by, still nervously looking around as if he were trying to find someone.

"Hello, Marvin," said Rufus. "Can you try to get the balloon down? You are much taller than me."

Marvin climbed onto the chair and grabbed the balloon. He squeezed it flat, as if it were a Chinese lantern, and the light went out.

"What do you need it for?" Marvin asked.

"Holly thought it was a sun," said Rufus. "She has never seen a magic balloon."

Marvin's face lit up and a big smile ran across his face. "Holly?" he asked. "Where is she? I've been looking for her all night long."

"Right in front of you, you mole head," said Brian. "Where else do you think she is?"

Marvin glanced at Holly. His mouth dropped open and he stuttered, "H-h-holly? Is that you?"

"Yeah," Holly said.

"I didn't even recognize you," said Marvin. "You look fantastic."

"Thanks," said Holly.

"And I thought you forgot about me," Marvin said.

"No, I didn't. Amanda just needed a bit longer than expected to give me a makeover," said Holly. "I'm sorry."

The rest of the evening turned out to be full of fun. They ate a lot, danced, and enjoyed the Christmas party. After a few hours, Holly got tired and told Marvin and her friends that she would be taking off. Since many students had left already, Brian, Rufus, and Amanda decided to go with her.

As they arrived back in Villa Nonesuch, Cookie was waiting for them, sitting in the recliner.

"Merry Christmas to you," he said. "Want to open your presents?"

The living room was filled with decorations. In the center was a fir tree so overloaded with tinsel and glass balls that it was hard to see any of its needles. Dozens of presents were stacked underneath.

Holly ran to her room and got the presents for her friends. When she returned, she opened Cookie's present first. She found a few pieces of a puzzle inside.

"You have to put it together to find out what your present really is," Cookie said.

Holly put the pieces together. It took her a while until she read the word "Whitespot."

"Your griffin?" Holly asked.

Cookie nodded. "He always liked you best. So I thought he'd be the perfect present for you. Amanda, Brian, and Rufus will get their own griffin so that you don't have to share Whitespot anymore."

Holly hugged the shape-shifter. She had always loved Whitespot, but she wouldn't have imagined in her wildest dreams that Cookie would part with him.

The next morning, Holly woke up early, feeling more excited than she had even been on Christmas morning—because maybe they would find the painting of the monastery of Chenaab in the Gallery of Wonders today. And that would mean she might be able to help Ileana now.

Holly went downstairs. To her surprise she found her friends already having breakfast.

"Good morning," Brian said, munching on a cookie.

"Let's go," Holly said.

"Don't you want to have breakfast first?" Amanda asked.

"Ileana gets weaker every day. I want to get to the gallery now," Holly said.

She grabbed a croissant and took off. Her friends followed.

Thirty minutes later, they entered the Gallery of Wonders.

The Experiment

Painting and writing take you to worlds unimagined. They move reality and fantasy closer together, and allow you to escape from reality for a while.

When Holly saw the many paintings in the gallery, she thought of her last adventure when Cuspidor had emptied the place. But she and her friends had been able to find the stolen paintings and bring them back. This time Holly was hoping to find that one painting they needed to get to the Golden Maple Tree.

"I'll check the upper floors," Brian said.

Holly joined Brian in climbing the double helix staircase that led upward, while Amanda and Rufus checked the lower levels.

Two hours later, Brian sat down on the staircase. "I didn't

find the painting," he complained.

Holly sat next to him. "Me neither."

Amanda and Rufus came walking up the staircase. The looks on their faces were not too promising.

"Nothing," Amanda said.

Rufus just shook his head. "We might as well go home now."

Disappointed, Holly nodded. Once again they had failed in their quest to help Ileana. Holly would have to go back to the infirmary and donate blood again, even though each time she did, it seemed to help less and less.

The following weeks, Holly used every free moment to sit alone on Whitespot's back and fly without any destination in mind over the island. Being high up in the sky freed her mind, and allowed her to get away from all the worries and think about other ways to get to the monastery.

One morning when school had started again, Holly and her friends headed for Creation and Deletion II class.

Holly dreaded it. Last school year she had failed to create anything but a flowerpot and one weird creature. Since then, she had not succeeded in creating much else. Professor LePawnee had assured her that the time would come and that she just needed practice. Nevertheless, that didn't help her now.

Gina, on the other hand, had already created dozens of things, and she was improving daily. She had created everything from a vase to a plant, but never a living being, as Holly had done with the flowerpot-Nukimai. Gina was still angry about that.

A squawk filled the air as Holly entered the classroom.

A flock of Chandrills were pecking from the outside at a window.

"This should be the last flock of Chandrills this year," Professor LePawnee said. "In just a few more weeks, the cold will have killed them off."

"But they'll be back in spring," Holly said.

"And probably there will be more than ever," Professor LePawnee added, sighing.

Discouraged, Holly sat down at her desk. She started to practice painting a table, but all she got out of her brush was a disappointing spark. "If I can't make this stupid brush work, I'm going to give up," she said.

"Nonsense," said Brian. "If I can do it, you can do it." He swung his brush and painted a gray table the size of a cup. It set down gently on the desk in front of them.

"All right," mumbled Brian. "I've still got a size problem, but at least it works."

Amanda leaned over from the desk behind them. "Look at this." She swung her brush, and a beige table with red spots formed.

"You learned to apply color already?" Brian asked.

"It really isn't that difficult," said Amanda. "I remembered the exact color, and now I just think of it when I make the brushstroke."

Holly frowned. Wasn't a Gindar supposed to be better than anybody else? So why couldn't she create anything? Maybe there was a mistake. Maybe she wasn't a Gindar. She felt nauseated by the success around her. She slammed her brush on the desk and leaned back, crossing her arms over her chest.

"Professssor LePawnee," shouted Gina. "Look what I've done."

The class gathered around Gina's desk. LePawnee pushed through the students and stared, speechless, at a cucumber-like creature with tiny arms, feet, and eyes. It blinked at the professor and started making faces.

"Th−th−this is incredible," stuttered Professor LePawnee. "You really created a creature?"

The class applauded.

Gina grinned at the professor and then looked straight at Holly. "I guess the oracle Gullveig underestimated me. Everyone will now see that I have amazing talents. I'm the Gindar, not Holly."

Holly felt devastated. Not only was Gina much better at creating things, but now she had proved herself a Gindar as well.

The bell rang. Holly dumped her belongings into her backpack. Tenshi grunted as she dropped a book on his head. She left the classroom without saying a word.

The next subject was Unfinished Painting II with Professor Farouche. Holly trudged to the vaulted classroom in the cellar. Brian followed her.

"What am I doing wrong?" Holly whined at Brian. "I can't create anything, I have bad grades in Farouche's class, and I can't even find this stupid monastery painting. I might not even be the Gindar they've been looking for. Maybe it is Gina."

"I'm sure it'll come," said Brian. "Some people are late bloomers."

"Yeah? How late? When I'm dead?" cried Holly. She

opened the massive metal door to Farouche's classroom. Holly noticed how Tenshi nervously bounced up and down in her backpack.

Last year, Farouche had used a Nukimai as a guinea pig for one of his experiments. Ever since, Tenshi had been afraid of the professor. Nevertheless, Holly had learned a great deal from Farouche. She found out that Grandpa Nikolas was the artist who had failed to complete the Unfinished, and ever since then they had struggled to become finished paintings.

"Welcome, class," announced Professor Farouche. "Today, I have a special treat for you—a new experiment." His thin lips tightened and a grin stole over his face. "You will be practicing on each other."

Acrylans

Besides painting and writing, there are other areas where fantasy and reality can mix.

There was deadly silence in the classroom. Holly felt a tremble as Tenshi winced and gently pulled up the zipper from inside the backpack. Holly began sweating. Knowing how much Professor Farouche disliked her, she thought he would surely pick her first. She slid partially under the desk, trying to make herself shorter and less noticeable.

Professor Farouche paced back and forth between the aisles. "Unfinished have many secrets that are still to be discovered. For example, Unfinished can enter a mindless body and use it for their purposes." He stopped in front of Holly's desk. "You can tell us more about this."

Confused, Holly stared at Farouche.

"Didn't your friend Ileana experience something like that?" he asked.

Holly remembered how Ileana had entered the body of the robin and attacked them. She nodded.

"Tell the class," Professor Farouche said.

Unwillingly, Holly stood up. She did not feel comfortable telling the story. It was nothing she wanted to remember. But she also did not want to get detention again. So she briefly told the class how horrible it was to see Ileana falling apart and how she had entered the body of the robin.

"And that is why you have to watch out," explained Professor Farouche after Holly was done. "Unfinished tend to stay close to the Wall of Gors. They know that their chances are better to catch an empty body there. Be observant around the Gors. Any animal that had its mind destroyed by the Gors could act as vessel for an unfinished mind."

"What happens if two Unfinished want the same body, or blood from the same person?" asked Serafina Abbey from the back row.

"Good question. Does anybody have an answer?"

Rufus raised his hand.

"Mr. Findley. Do you know?" asked Farouche, leaning menacingly over Brian's desk.

Brian bit his lip and shook his head. Rufus cleared his throat to attract attention, but Farouche ignored him.

"No? Of course you wouldn't know that," said Farouche. "What about you, Ms. O'Flanigan?"

Holly shook her head.

"And you, Ms. Heavenlock?"

Amanda shrugged.

"Hasn't anybody studied the books I gave you last year?"

Rufus fidgeted. He jumped up from his bench. "I know it, Professor."

Farouche's lips tightened and his eyes became slits. "Have I asked you if you know it?"

Rufus sat back down.

"Usually, the two Unfinished would fight until they are exhausted," said Farouche. "Let's say Unfinished One drains a creature's blood, and let's say Unfinished Two also wants this blood. Then, Unfinished Two will attack Unfinished One. Do you know what would happen next?"

Professor Farouche paced through the aisles again. "I will tell you what would happen," he said. "The blood would continue through Unfinished One to Unfinished Two. Unfinished One would realize he's losing the blood he had just drained. He would try to get it back and would concentrate on Unfinished Two. This is the chance for a victim to escape. When the two Unfinished are focused on each other."

Farouche walked to the end of the room where some cauldrons were stacked up on a shelf. Next to them were many glass tubes with compartments inside them. Professor Farouche picked them up.

"But let's get started with the experiment," he said, grinning. "All blood contains so-called acrylans. There are Gindar, Legumer, Tracer, and Regular acrylans. Every person has each type inside his body. It depends on the amount of each type you have whether you will be a Gindar, Legumer, Tracer, or not a painter at all."

"So our creative talent lies in our blood?" Serafina Abbey asked.

"Partly yes," explained Farouche. "An adult can simply take a blood test, and he will know what kind of painter he is, but children are a different story. You are still developing your skills. That's why the amount of acrylans is not fixed. Study and practice can increase the amount of one type or another. So a Tracer might develop into a Legumer, and vice versa. But once you have passed puberty, you can't change what you are anymore. That's why you are at a crucial age."

Professor Farouche handed out a glass tube to each student. "This experiment will track what changes your blood undergoes in the next couple of weeks. I will pair you off, and each week, your partner will take a blood sample from you and store it in one of the compartments of the glass tube. By spring you will have many samples, and then we will analyze how your blood has changed and what kind of painter you are most likely to become."

After the professor had handed out the tubes, he paired the students off with their neighbors. Holly was teamed with Rufus.

Farouche showed how to draw blood and store it in the tiny compartments of the glass vials. A few minutes later, the students were practicing on their partners.

Rufus swung his brush, made the necessary brushstroke, and a thread of white paint appeared between Holly's wrists and the glass tube. A few drops of blood crawled along the white paint into the compartment, and the thread dissolved.

Holly felt sick to her stomach. She thought of her weekly

blood donations and then she remembered how Cuspidor had drawn her blood last year. She had almost died back then. Dizzy, she closed her eyes.

Gate Paintings II

Films and computer games are other areas besides painting and writing where fantasy becomes part of everyday life.

"I am done," Rufus said.

Holly opened her eyes again. It wasn't as bad as she had expected it. There were only a few drops of blood in the compartment, nothing compared to what Cuspidor had sucked out of her body or what she had been donating during the weekly blood transfusions. Holly performed the same procedure on Rufus, and within a few minutes they had completed their tasks.

"Time for you to read up on acrylans," Farouche said. "Open your books to page fourteen."

In the following weeks, the procedure became a routine.

They first drew each other's blood and then had to read up on certain topics.

By February, Rufus and Holly had collected quite a bit of each other's blood. Winter had finally killed the Chandrills and the skies had become quiet. Cliffony lay solemnly under a five-foot layer of snow. By that time not much was left of Ileana, besides a few outlines and some pieces of flesh. Holly was desperate. Would she have to watch her friend dissolve completely?

March came and went, and all Holly did was search the Gallery of Wonders for the monastery painting. Occasionally, she heard Cuspidor's voice, but it was not as frequent anymore. Everything else, however, was going well. She had even created a dining table in Creation and Deletion II. It had two legs and fell over when set down, but Holly didn't care. At least she had created something.

Amanda spent her time focusing on Aqua-inking and Color Painting I. Her Aqua-inking skills had improved because she had received private lessons from Professor Bundo. Apart from these classes, she developed her hobby of mixing creams and powders in Villa Nonesuch's kitchen.

By April, they had finally checked every single painting in the Gallery of Wonders and come to the conclusion that the Q woman must have been wrong. There was no painting of the monastery of Chenaab anywhere to be found.

Holly sat down between Rufus and Brian on the double helix staircase.

"Have you checked the tenth floor?" Brian asked.

"I did," Holly said. "Nothing there. Just like on all the other

floors."

"I do not think the painting is in here," said Rufus, pulling out a carrot from his bag. "Want one?"

Brian made a face. "Yuck."

Rufus broke off a piece and fed it to Shardee, who was nestled on his shoulder. "Even Shardee eats carrots."

"But that is not a normal bird," said Brian. "It's not even a normal Chandrill. Why didn't it die when the winter came? All the other Chandrills did."

"Shardee is not one of them," said Rufus reproachfully. "He is very sophisticated and has the same taste as I have."

Brian rolled his eyes. "How can a bird be sophisticated? It's just a stupid animal."

Holly jumped up, interrupting the conversation that was surely about to lead to another fight.

"Gate Paintings II will start soon," she said. "We should go to the classroom."

"We can just stay here," said Brian. "Professor Hubbleworth said we would have the class in the Gallery of Wonders today."

"Oh, that's right," Holly said. "I guess she wouldn't give us detention for not meeting in the classroom anyhow. She's become so easy-going. In Donkleywood she really hated kids, but here she seems to like them. I just don't understand why she still doesn't remember that she's from Donkleywood."

The double doors to the Gallery of Wonders opened, and a crowd of students walked in, trailed by Professor Hubbleworth and two girls who helped her carry books.

"So here you are," said the professor. "Didn't I tell you

that we'd meet in the classroom and then go to the gallery together?"

"I'm sorry, Professor," Holly said.

Hubbleworth led the crowd to a corner of the gallery.

"Everybody please gather around," she said and clapped her hands.

Bats fluttered down, carrying two paintings with them. The professor leaned the paintings against a wall. For months, they had studied theory and learned about different worlds. Today was the day that they were about to get to know these worlds first-hand.

"There are two types of gate paintings," said Hubbleworth. "One type allows you to travel between two locations within one world, and the other leads you into other worlds."

She pointed at the painting on the right. It showed a landscape where every tree and bush had the color blue. In the distance, picturesque houses with red-shingled roofs indicated that people lived close by.

"This is the land of Lardee," said the professor. "It is another world." She turned to the painting on the left, showing a meadow in the forest. "This, on the other hand, is another location in our world. It's a place in the Land of Cuspidor."

Hubbleworth clapped her hands and the bats carried the painting of the meadow away.

"We will focus on this painting and we will enter the world of Lardee today," said the professor. "But we will stay only a few minutes."

She swung her brush and opened the painting. The aisle in the gallery filled with bright light. The students fidgeted. Some

chewed their fingernails, while others paced up and down.

"This is so exciting," said Billy, the Ledesma boy standing next to Holly.

"Not really," muttered Holly, remembering how she had stepped through a gate painting a few times already.

"Follow me," said Hubbleworth, stepping into the lights.

Holly followed and came out in world that looked as if someone had spilled blue paint over the entire landscape.

"This painting is going to get us back to Magora," said Hubbleworth, placing a miniature painting on the ground. She swung her brush and opened it.

Just after the last student had stepped into the land of Lardee, the professor chased the first students back into the Gallery of Wonders though the other gate.

"Time to go back," she said, "you need to learn some more things before the class ends."

After they all had returned safely to the gallery, Hubbleworth said, "So now that you have experienced how it is when a painting opens, I want each of you to practice it."

She waved Rufus to her side. "Mr. Letterhead, you have been one of my best students. I want you to open a gate." The professor pointed at a painting on the wall, which featured a red meadow with green cows.

Rufus swung his brush with ease. The image vanished and a gate opened up.

"Very well done," Ms. Hubbleworth said.

The professor picked up a chair and threw it into the lights. As if hitting a glass wall, the chair bounced off and fell to the floor.

Holly flinched. What had just happened?

"Can anyone explain why this chair didn't go through the gate?" Hubbleworth asked.

Billy, the Ledesma boy raised his hand.

"Yes, Mr. Dinroad," said the professor.

"Because objects can't be transported through gate paintings," said Billy. "They are only for people."

Holly knew that this could not be. She had learned last year from Professor LePawnee that gate paintings were used to supply Magora with goods.

"Not quite right, Mr. Dinroad," said Hubbleworth. "Objects have to be about the size of a hand to pass through a gate, and they have to be carried on the body."

"So what if you want to get something like a chair through the gate?" Billy asked.

"You would have to take the chair apart and take the individual pieces with you," explained Hubbleworth. "But it isn't only big objects that can't get through—some people also cannot get through the gate."

"Really?" Holly asked, raising her hand. "Who?"

"Unconscious people," said Professor Hubbleworth. "They behave like objects. And anything that is connected to either an unconscious person or an object cannot get through the gate."

"So if I tried to carry someone unconscious to the other side, I wouldn't be able to cross?" Holly asked.

"Correct," said the professor. "The same thing happens when you hold an object in your hand. Try it!"

Hubbleworth handed Holly the chair and pointed at the

gate. Holly picked it up and walked right toward the lights. With a bang she stumbled back, tripped, and fell to the ground. It was as if she had hit a glass wall.

"Are you okay?" the professor asked.

Holly nodded.

"See," Hubbleworth said, "You can't enter as long as you hold on to that chair."

Holly was about to get up when she saw four rings attached to the floor tiles next to her.

"Excuse me, Professor," said Holly. "What are these rings for?" She pointed at them.

"Just decoration," said Hubbleworth, turning away from Holly. "I will see you next week at the same time right here." The professor departed down the aisle, and a few minutes later the class had dispersed.

Holly got up and put the chair back where it belonged. The bats fluttered down again and carried the gate painting away.

"These rings must be more than just decoration," said Rufus. "Why would anyone put rings on the floor?"

Holly nodded. She found it quite odd.

"You think there's something hidden underneath?" Brian asked.

Holly and Brian gently pulled on two of the rings. Nothing happened.

"Take the other two," Holly said.

Rufus and Amanda picked up the other two rings and pulled. The tile began to budge. They pulled harder. A latch sprang open, and a narrow staircase led down into the ground.

"I think we found something," said Holly, illuminating her

brush.

She climbed down into darkness. When they reached the bottom, they found a prison cell with a heavy lock at the door.

Holly put her brush between the bars and illuminated the cell behind it.

"Holy smokes," said Brian. "Can you believe this?" He pressed his face between the bars to get a better look.

There were eight niches all around the prison cell. In each one an easel had been set up. Large paintings stood on them, covered with white cloths. Above each niche were signs. Everything was covered with cobwebs.

"It's a secret gallery," Holly said, excited.

"And I think we have finally found what we have been looking for," said Rufus, pointing at one of the paintings.

A large sign dangled on one screw above one of the niches. The paint had peeled off, and it looked as if it had been there for ages. Excited, Holly read out loud what was written there: "Monastery of Chenaab."

The Monastery of Chenaab

In other fields of creativity, like movies, the viewer enters another world for a limited period of time, just like during reading and painting.

The painting on the easel in the niche was covered with a white cloth. On the side, Holly could see a lavishly-carved golden frame peeking out.

"We have to get inside there," said Holly, pulling on the heavy lock on the cell.

Amanda took out her hairpin and began picking the lock.

Brian shook his head. "I think we have to get a bolt cutter to open that."

"You are not going to break in," Rufus said. "This is a criminal act. I am not going to help you with this."

"Just how are you going to stop us?" Brian asked.

"I will report you," Rufus said.

"You wouldn't," Brian said.

"Forget it," Amanda said, pulling out the hairpin. "It doesn't open anyhow."

"All right," said Holly. "Let's leave and think about how we can open it."

After they had all climbed out of the opening in the floor, Holly pushed the hatch shut.

"Who do you think might have the key?" Amanda asked.

"I don't know if anybody has it," said Brian. "It looks as if it has not been used in ages. But if anybody would have it, it would be Professor LePawnee—she's the headmistress, after all."

"You are very correct, Mr. Findley," echoed a voice through the gallery.

They spun around. Hands on her hips, Professor Hubbleworth stepped out from behind a large painting. "Professor LePawnee keeps the key in her office. It is attached to a key ring that hangs in the wall closet next to the window."

"Why are you telling us all this?" Rufus asked.

"I'm just trying to help," Hubbleworth said.

Holly couldn't make sense of it all. Just a few minutes ago, the professor had told her the rings were there for decoration purposes only, and now she acted as if she knew what was down there—and even told them where they could find the key. Could it be that even after all this time, the MSP still had a weird effect on her mind?

"And do you actually want us to steal the key, or what?" Amanda asked. "You, a professor?"

"It's up to you what you do with this information," said

Ms. Hubbleworth. "As long as you don't tell anyone you got it from me."

Just like Amanda, Holly found Ms. Hubbleworth's reaction quite strange, but before she could say something the professor continued.

"Not many people know this, but Professor LePawnee has a guard," said Ms. Hubbleworth. "It's a brownie as big as a thimble. He hides in the closet and protects the keys. So watch out."

"What are you getting out of this?" Rufus asked, still skeptical.

"Don't ask too many questions." The professor turned around and walked off.

Once Hubbleworth was away at a safe distance, Rufus turned to Holly. "I don't trust her. There's something odd about this whole story. Why would she tell us all this? I think she wants us to get caught stealing the key."

"But we have no choice," said Brian. "Otherwise we won't get to the monastery."

"And we need to get to the monastery to save Ileana," said Holly. "The leaves of the Golden Maple Tree could save her."

"We have six weeks left until the school year is over," said Rufus. "Do not get us expelled. We need to focus on our studies. Exams will start in four weeks."

"Forget about exams," Holly said, walking toward the exit. "Ileana's life is at stake." She turned to Brian and Amanda. "But Rufus is right about one thing—we don't want to get expelled, so we have to develop a plan to get the key first. We can act later."

The next few weeks Holly was busy researching not only magical creatures like brownies but also practicing creation and healing brushstrokes—anything that was useful in her quest to help Ileana.

The snow had finally melted and spring arrived. The large poplars around Cliffony turned a lush green, while the sun filled the cafeteria with bright light, but Holly couldn't enjoy it. She couldn't forget that every passing day brought Ileana closer to completely dissolving.

"Do you know all the numbers?" asked Brian one day, flipping through his Color Painting I study book while chewing on a piece of chocolate.

"I know a few," said Holly, picking through her potato salad with a fork as she turned the pages of a book on magical creatures. "I can't seem to concentrate on the exams."

Rufus and Amanda walked through the cafeteria with their trays in hand.

Amanda peered over Holly's shoulder. "And? Have you found anything?"

"You had better focus on the exam," said Rufus. "The first one is in five days."

"I know," said Holly. "I have to get those out of the way so I can focus on a plan to trick LePawnee's brownie."

Holly studied day and night until the exams were over. She felt quite confident that she had passed them all except Unfinished Painting II.

After the last test, Holly stepped out of Professor Farouche's classroom. "Done!" she shouted, excited. "That's it."

"That was not fair," complained Rufus, trudging after Holly. "He gave us questions that are purely theoretical. The answers depend on which theory you support and not on facts."

"Who cares?" said Holly. "It's over. Now we can focus on the brownie."

She headed for the library, trailed by Amanda and Brian.

"Aren't you coming, Rufus?" asked Amanda. "We have to get the key."

"I am not going to break into LePawnee's office," Rufus said.

"But what about Ileana?" Holly asked.

"You cannot just go around and break into someone's place. What if they catch you?"

"I don't care if they catch me," said Holly. "We can save Ileana's life, and I will do whatever it takes to help her. Besides, have you noticed that there are more Chandrills every day?" She pointed through a stained-glass window at the sky that was filled with Chandrills. "If we don't find the Golden Maple Tree, the whole island will be in danger. People are starting to be afraid of going outside."

"But there are rules, and you just cannot go around breaking them as you see fit," said Rufus. He muttered in disagreement and headed in the other direction.

"Chicken," said Brian. "He would only slow us down anyway."

"But he knows more than the three of us together," said Holly. "And he's still our friend. Remember what we promised when we came to Magora?"

"We are in this together," Brian repeated their vow. "Yeah,

I know. But we can't force him to help us."

They headed down the corridor to the library.

"Did anyone find something on brownies?" Holly asked.

"I found a book called *Everything you always wanted to know about brownies*," said Amanda. "But the book is for reference only. It can't be checked out."

"Do you think you can find it again?" asked Holly.

Amanda nodded.

They entered Cliffony's library. Holly glanced up at the bookshelves that lined the wood-paneled walls. Staircases led up to the second floor balcony.

"I think I saw it up there," said Amanda, pointing at an antique cupboard.

Holly followed her friends upstairs. Amanda pulled the doors open. A loud squeak echoed through the library. A few students briefly looked up from the study desk.

Amanda pointed at a thin book on the fifth shelf. "That's the one."

Holly pulled it out and flipped it open. She turned to the table of contents.

"This is exactly what I've been looking for." She pointed to the sixth line on the page.

It read, "Brownies and Their Weaknesses." Holly turned to page 94 and read aloud, "Recent studies have unveiled that brownies have two weaknesses. There are two kinds of food that make brownies do almost anything: Comerian eggs—"

"What are Comerian eggs?" interrupted Brian.

Amanda and Holly shrugged.

"If Rufus were here, he would know," Amanda said.

"Let me finish." Holly continued reading, "Comerian eggs and banana cakes."

"Banana cakes?" repeated Amanda. "Why banana cakes?"

"I guess they just like them," said Holly, slamming the book shut. "I think I've got a plan now."

"Are you going to lure him with a banana cake, and then catch him with a butterfly net?" Brian asked, laughing

"Yeah, right," said Amanda. "The moment we catch the brownie, he'll scream and the whole school will know what's going on."

Holly shook her head and headed out of the library. "I've got a much better plan." She headed directly for Professor LePawnee's office. "Stay here and wait."

She knocked at the door, which was flanked by two shiny silver suits of armor.

"Come in," Professor LePawnee's voice echoed from inside.

Holly walked in and plunged into the soft armchair in front of the headmistress' desk.

"How can I help you?" she asked.

Holly didn't know what she should talk about. She had only come to check and see if the brownie was around, but she had to ask the professor something. And there was one thing that Holly had long wanted to know more about anyway.

"I'm still wondering about Cuspidor's daughter," began Holly. "What if she does exist—and I am her?"

Professor LePawnee glided around her desk and put both her hands on Holly's shoulders. "There are millions of books out there. Because one book states something, doesn't mean it is the truth."

Holly nodded. "I still wonder sometimes."

"You shouldn't waste your time thinking about this. Now that the exams are over you should enjoy yourself. Spend some time with your friends, play around, and discover new things before you return to Donkleywood."

"You know, I have discovered something new," Holly said. "I'm baking a lot. I enjoy making—" she raised her voice, "banana cakes." She stood up from the armchair. "Yes, I really enjoy baking banana cakes. Banana cakes taste great. You should come over to Villa Nonesuch one day and taste my banana cake."

Each time Holly raised her voice to say "banana cake" she heard a tiny sigh in the closet. "Just yesterday I made three different banana cakes, and this afternoon we'll eat them. Would you like to come?"

"I would love to come, but I have to correct your exams," said Professor LePawnee. "Maybe some other time."

"Okay," said Holly, smiling. "Then we'll have the banana cakes all to ourselves. They are sitting right now in Villa Nonesuch's kitchen."

"Enjoy," LePawnee said.

As Holly left the office, she heard another sigh from the closet

"The brownie must have heard that," said Brian as Holly came out. "Even without eavesdropping at the door, we would have heard the words 'banana cake' three miles away."

Holly and her friends hid behind the suit of armor. "Now we just have to wait until Professor LePawnee goes home,"

said Holly. "Then we will see if the brownie heads off to Villa Nonesuch."

They didn't have to wait long until LePawnee left the office. Before she pulled the door shut, she whispered, "And take good care of everything, Ogniwarf."

A faint voice replied, "Don't worry."

A few moments later, the door opened a crack and a brownie as small as a mouse peeked out. He balanced a spiked hat between his pointy ears, which held the hat in place. Underneath a beaten-up leather vest, he wore a green shirt and a pink bowtie. His large feet were wrapped in bags tied around the ankles with shoelaces.

Holly put her index finger on her lips. She held her breath as the brownie pulled the door shut and tiptoed down the corridor.

"I knew he couldn't resist," Holly whispered.

As soon as Ogniwarf had disappeared, Holly went into the office and headed directly to the closet. A large keychain hung prominently inside. Holly grabbed the chain and ran out of the room, trailed by Brian and Amanda.

"What if we don't make it back by the time Ogniwarf finds out there is no banana cake?" Amanda asked.

"We just have to be back before him," replied Holly, speeding down the corridor. She veered around the corner and had just passed the library when a siren went off.

"I think we've been discovered," Holly said.

Kidnapping

It all depends on the movie whether the viewer enters an entirely new world or an aspect of the real world.

The sound of the siren was deafening. Students started to come out of the classrooms, filling the corridors. Holly maneuvered around the students and turned at a corner.

She almost knocked over a man who was standing there. But Holly was able to stop just a few inches in front of him. However, Brian and Amanda ran full speed into Holly. They all fell forward to the ground as the man jumped out of the way.

"Can't you watch where you are going?" Professor Farouche asked.

He was out of breath and had a serious look on his face.

"I'm really sorry," Holly said, hoping that Farouche would not suspect that they had set off the siren. "Why did the alarm go off?" she asked, trying to sound innocent.

"Ileana has been kidnapped," Professor Farouche replied.

"What?" Holly shouted, jumping back up onto her feet.

They hadn't set off the alarm. This was about Ileana. But who would kidnap an Unfinished? Ileana was about to die. Kidnapping her did not really make sense.

"What happened?" Brian asked.

"Professor Kasmera was going to check on Ileana when she saw something really odd," Farouche said. "Professor Hubbleworth had Ileana in her arms and was escaping through a window."

Holly could not believe what she heard. Ms. Hubbleworth had been acting very strangely all year. Sometimes she behaved as if she hated kids, and sometimes she was very friendly. It almost seemed as if she had a split personality. But even at her worst, the professor did not seem capable of kidnapping.

"Then what happened?" Amanda asked.

"Professor Kasmera ran to the window and looked out. She saw that Professor Hubbleworth had tied Ileana to a griffin. She was unconscious. Next thing, they were flying away toward the Griffin Hatchery. Kasmera chased after them."

Holly turned to Brian and Amanda. "We have to find Ileana. Let's go," she said, and they took off toward the exit.

They squeezed themselves through a crowd of students that was now blocking the corridors, loudly chattering about what had just happened. Holly darted down the staircase that led to Papplewick Street and ran right into Professor Kasmera.

Sweat was dripping from the professor's forehead and tears were running down her cheeks.

"It's worse than we thought," she yelped. "Joline broke into Villa Nonesuch."

"Oh, no," Holly gulped. "Are Rufus and Villa Nonesuch okay?"

At that moment, Kaplin and Farouche appeared and LePawnee landed her griffin at the bottom of the stairs.

"I am so glad you are here, Leguthiandra," said Professor Kasmera. "Something horrible has just happened."

LePawnee jumped off her griffin and took Kasmera in her arms. "Relax, Cynthia. Tell us what happened."

Kasmera sat down on the stairs, wiping off her tears.

"When I saw Joline kidnap Ileana, I followed them to the Griffin Hatchery. By the time I got there, Joline had already broken the door of Villa Nonesuch. She has kidnapped Rufus as well."

Holly's heart began to pound as if it were about to break through her ribs. Two of her best friends were in danger because of Ms. Hubbleworth.

Amanda put her arm around Holly.

"And how is Villa Nonesuch doing?" Brian asked.

"I talked to her, but she doesn't remember everything," said Kasmera. "She was hurt badly. Professor Hubbleworth had set explosives at the door and blew it open."

Holly was shocked by the violence the professor had displayed. Hubbleworth had been unfriendly at times but never violent.

"What does Villa Nonesuch remember?" Professor LePawnee asked.

"She remembers that Joline wanted something from Rufus,

but she doesn't remember what it was," said Kasmera. "Rufus didn't give it to her, and so she knocked him out."

"Does the tree house know where they went?" LePawnee asked.

"Yes," said Kasmera. "Villa Nonesuch said they wanted to fly to the monastery of Chenaab."

Holly listened carefully. She had been looking for the monastery of Chenaab all this time. Maybe Hubbleworth was trying to take Ileana to the Golden Maple Tree to save her. But why would she attack Rufus and kidnap Ileana then? If she wanted to get Ileana to the maple to save her, she could have talked to the other professors and they would have helped her.

Brian pulled Holly and Amanda a few steps away from the professors.

"Why would Ms. Hubbleworth need a griffin to fly to the land of Cuspidor?" Brian whispered to Holly. "She knows more than any of us about gate paintings. She could have just opened a gate to the land of Cuspidor."

"Remember what we've learned in Gate Painting II?" said Holly. "Unconscious people can't pass through gates. She couldn't have taken Rufus and Ileana if they were unconscious. Ms. Hubbleworth must have planned this long ago."

Professor Kasmera wiped her eyes. "If I had come just a few minutes earlier, I could have stopped it all."

"It is not your fault," said LePawnee, sitting down next to her.

"How could she pass the Wall of Gors?" Farouche asked.

"It was unbelievable," said Kasmera. "Villa Nonesuch said

that Joline tied the unconscious children to the griffin and flew right into a swarm of Giraflies, which covered their entire bodies. Then she flew into a cloud of Chandrills. When she reached the Wall of Gors, she was able to pass right through with them."

"You're right," Amanda said to Holly. "She did plan it all. It's exactly what the Giraflies do. They hide inside the Chandrills when they cross the Wall of Gors."

"Right," said Holly, "and Ms. Hubbleworth surrounded herself with Chandrills. It must have the same effect as hiding inside one of them, and so the Gors couldn't register their minds."

"If Ms. Hubbleworth took off to the land of Cuspidor, she must be a spy for the Unfinished," Holly said. "Then it would make sense that she wanted to take Ileana to her fellow Unfinished. But why Rufus?"

Brian and Amanda shrugged.

"Whatever she has planned, we have to get Rufus and Ileana back." Holly said, heading down the stairs.

She waved at Brian and Amanda to follow her, while she watched the professors talking with each other. They were so occupied with themselves they would not even notice if Holly and her friends took off.

"Let's go," said Holly. "We have the keys and we know where the painting of the monastery is."

They ran down the corridors through the crowd of students and entered the Gallery of Wonders. Holly headed directly for the hatch. She pulled it open and climbed down, followed by Brian and Amanda.

"Try the keys," said Amanda, lifting the heavy lock.

Holly sifted through the keys on the ring. After the fourth try, she found the right one. The gate to the secret gallery swung open with a squeak.

Holly raced straight to the niche with the sign reading, "Monastery of Chenaab," then pulled the white linen to the side.

The painting showed an image of an old monastery overgrown with ivy. Towering poplars lined the high walls. The main building overlooking the walls was built out of black stone. Apart from the color, it reminded Holly of one of the buildings in Tuscany she had seen on TV.

Holly stepped closer to the painting and took out her brush. "That's it," she said. "I'll try to open it."

She swung her brush and paint shot out of the tip, hitting the picture. Every particle of the painting brightened up. Within a second, they were standing in front of a wall of lights.

"Are you ready?" Holly glanced at Brian and Amanda on either side of her.

They nodded, took each other's hands, and stepped into the painting.

The Monks

Games can be like books, movies, or paintings. They take the player away from reality.

Hundreds of lights zoomed past Holly as she stepped into the painting. She smiled, remembering that these lights were Sylkies.

Then, everything went dark and Holly landed on a hill. Dozens of poplars cast an eerie shadow onto the monastery that lay in front of her. A cold wind was blowing. Holly took out her knitted cap from her pocket and pulled it over her head.

"It doesn't look very inviting," Brian said.

"Let's hope it's not full of Unfinished," said Holly. She tried to open the door, but it didn't budge.

"What now?" Amanda asked. "We'd better not knock. I

don't think we are welcome here."

Brian strolled along the high wall and vanished behind a corner. "I think we might be able to climb over the wall," he shouted a few seconds later. "It's much lower here." He peered out from behind the corner and waved at them.

Holly and Amanda followed him. The wall was only about six feet high where Brian was standing. He dragged a tree trunk to the wall, climbed up, and jumped down on the other side.

Holly followed him. When she reached the top, she looked down into a garden. Poison ivy was everywhere. Upon closer examination, Holly noticed that the plants concealed dozens of tombstones. Many of them had fallen over and were spattered with mud. Holly jumped down.

"Yuck," said Amanda from the top of the wall. "They could at least add some color to this place. A little cobalt blue on the stones would give them a brighter look."

"It's a cemetery," said Brian, "not a glitter world."

Holly headed for the entrance of the monastery. The door was wide open. She peeked inside a long, dark entrance hall with gargoyles staring at her from all sides and stepped inside.

"What's that smell?" Amanda asked, wrinkling her nose.

"Smells like rotten meat," said Holly. It almost made her vomit. She pulled her sweater over her nose.

They tiptoed to another door at the end of the entrance hall.

Just as Holly reached for the knob, the door flew open. They all jumped behind a pillar. A procession of monks marched in.

Their brown cloaks were pulled low over their faces. They

hummed and moved rhythmically to their singsong melody. The last monk carried a cauldron with bread inside. He set it on the ground, breathing heavily. He rested for a second while the procession continued to a small opening where a staircase led downward.

"I always have to do all the nasty work," mumbled the monk. He pulled his hood slightly back and glanced over his shoulder at the door.

Holly covered her mouth with her hand. What she saw was horrible. Brian gulped and stopped breathing, while Amanda bit her fingernails.

The monk had no face. His two eyeballs hovered in mid-air. Blood vessels hung like seaweed from the eyeballs, and blood dripped from the end of the veins down into his cloak. Pencil lines whirled around the eyeballs, outlining his head and his mouth. He turned back to the procession and stumbled after the other monks.

"Did you see that?" asked Amanda. "You could see inside his head."

"Unfinished," whispered Brian. "Now we know what happened to the monks of the monastery. Cuspidor must have turned them into Unfinished by sucking out their blood."

"We'd better follow them," said Holly. "They might lead us to Rufus and Ileana."

Holly waited a minute and then tiptoed along the wall to the staircase. The monks had disappeared into the cellar. Trying not to make noise, Holly descended the stairs. There was barely any light, but she didn't dare illuminate her brush for fear the Unfinished would see them. At the bottom of the stairs, Holly found herself in a cellar with roughly-carved limestone columns. She sat down on the stairs and stared at the many archways that led out of the hall.

"Bummer, we missed them," said Holly. "Where do we go now?"

Brian and Amanda walked around, checking out the place, while Holly wondered where the monks might have gone and why they had used a cauldron to carry bread.

A few minutes passed when she suddenly heard the singsong voices again.

"They're coming back," said Amanda. "I can hear them chanting."

She jumped up and flung herself behind one of the columns. Holly and Brian sped after Amanda and crouched next to her.

The procession returned and passed their hiding place. Holly peeked out from behind the column. The last monk was still carrying the cauldron, but it was no longer filled with bread. Holly leaned forward and saw a thick, red liquid. She sniffed and immediately covered her nose with her hand, as she had the sudden urge to throw up. The cauldron was filled to the top with blood.

What was going on? Holly did not understand. Where did all this blood come from? She had a sudden horrible thought: what if the blood had come from Rufus? But surely so much blood couldn't have come from him alone. Hopefully, he was still alive.

The monks walked up the stairs. After the chant had faded into the distance, Holly went down the aisle from where the

monks had appeared. On both sides were prison cells.

"This must be the dungeon," Amanda said.

Holly looked through the bars into one of the cells. About fifty men with long beards were lying motionless on the floor. They all looked like barely-living skeletons.

Holly peeked into the next cell. More men lay on the damp floor. "I think I know what this place is," she said.

"What?" Amanda asked in a harsh whisper.

"I think this is a blood bank for the Unfinished," said Holly. "They keep humans here so they can take their blood."

Brian and Amanda were silent, staring at the many cells around them.

"They might have locked Rufus up in here," said Holly. "We have to check the place."

They went from cell to cell, illuminating their brushes. But among all those bodies Holly didn't see Rufus. Either he was somewhere else or they had killed him already. Grief overcame Holly and tears welled up in her eyes. Then, she heard a faint voice.

"Please. Come here."

Holly went to one of the cells. A man with a long, brown beard was lying on his stomach and had propped himself up. "You've got to get out of here, or they will catch you," said the man.

Holly pulled at the bars of the door. "We might be able to get you out," she said.

"Don't worry about me," said the man. "You have to listen very carefully." He pulled himself up on the bars and stared at Holly face to face. "I was once the abbot of this monastery. It was a peaceful place—until he came along."

"Who?" Brian asked.

"Cuspidor," said the abbot. "He conquered the monastery and imprisoned us. The Unfinished took over and locked us in the dungeon. Ever since then they have been using us as blood donors. They feed us and keep us alive so that we produce fresh blood. Once we have recovered, they drain us again until most of us fall unconscious."

"We have to get you out of here," Holly said.

"That can wait," said the abbot. "The Unfinished won't kill us. They need our blood. What is more important is that you get to the center of the monastery."

"Why?" Amanda asked.

"The Golden Maple Tree is at the center of the monastery," said the abbot. "I think Cuspidor's plan is to overrun Magora with Chandrills. For hundreds of years we have been harvesting the tree. In spring, it develops blossoms that ripen into leaves, then turn into Chandrills. If you don't harvest them, the leaves will multiply each year and the Chandrills will increase. You have to get there and burn the tree."

"But it has healing powers," said Holly. "We can't just destroy the tree. It could help thousands."

"It can be of help if it's in the right hands," said the abbot. "But if it's in the wrong hands, it can destroy everything."

"All right," said Holly. "We'll take care of that, but then we'll come back and get you out of here." She turned around and ran down the hall. Brian and Amanda followed.

"Wait," the abbot shouted. "When you get to the tree, match the color of the entrance to the color wheel. Otherwise,

the island will sink."

Holly just nodded, not really understanding what the abbot had just told her. She kept running up the staircase to the entrance hall. The others followed her.

"What does matching the color of the entrance to the color wheel have to do with the island sinking?" Amanda asked.

Holly shook her head. "We'll see. First we have to find the tree."

They crossed the entrance hall and entered the same door through which the monks had come. They were standing in an open courtyard. Fifteen doors on each side led into the buildings. Stone benches, overgrown with ivy, stood between poplars.

On the opposite side of the courtyard was a golden gate. Sculptures of angels, peacocks, and elves were intertwined with carved maple leaves. The shadows of the moonlight cast upon the peacocks almost made them look as if they had come alive.

"Maybe that is the way to the center of the monastery," Holly said.

Amanda headed directly across the courtyard and halted right in front of the gate. "It's so beautiful, isn't it?" she said.

"I don't think we should be standing around here where anybody could see us," Brian said.

"He's right," said Holly, urging Amanda on.

Holly leaned against the gate and pushed hard. "Would you help me instead of standing there staring at the angels?"

Amanda and Brian threw themselves with all their weight against the golden gate. It slowly creaked open and dense fog blew out.

The Lake of Colors

Just like books and paintings, games can take people into a different world as well. Once people are in this world, the struggle begins not to let this fantasy world take over real life.

Holly could not see a single thing. She did not even know if there was a room, a hall, or only a corridor. Just as she was about to light up the tip of her brush to see more, she heard a door in the courtyard squeak open. Instinctively, she pushed Brian and Amanda into the fog. Before she could jump in herself, she saw the unfinished monk with the cauldron stepping out into the courtyard.

"Intruder!" he yelled as he saw Holly.

He stumbled forward and fell over his cloak. Other doors to the courtyard opened. Holly jumped into the fog and started running straight ahead.

"Brian? Amanda?" she shouted.

"Yes," their voices sounded somewhere in the distance. "We're ahead of you. Keep going and you'll see a light."

As she saw the light in the distance, Holly heard the monks' voices behind her.

She kept running. The fog thinned out and the outlines of Brian and Amanda became visible.

"The monk saw me," said Holly, breathlessly. "Keep running! They're after us."

But Brian and Amanda didn't budge.

"What are you waiting for? Why are you just standing around? Keep running," said Holly as she reached them.

Brian and Amanda didn't say a word. They pointed at what was in front of them. Holly looked through an opening in a wall and saw a big lake with squares of different-colored water. It reached up to the threshold of the hall. In the middle of it was an island with a building similar to that of the monastery, but in smaller size—like an annex. The crown of a tree peeked out from behind the thick brick walls.

"Is that the Golden Maple Tree?" Holly asked.

"Probably, but how are we going to get over there?" Brian asked.

Holly noticed a few Turapids peering out of the water. She climbed through the opening and headed for the lake.

"I think we just found the origins of Aqua-inking," said Holly, wiggling her finger in the water.

The Turapids paddled closer.

"Look," Holly said. "There's the lanteen, and there's the

brush." She pointed at the gate that led into the annex. A golden brush hung on a string in front of the gate. Next to it was a box. "I'll bet that the box will open up when we get enough points, just like in Aqua-inking."

"Catch them," echoed through the hallway.

Holly turned around. The monk came running through the fog, followed by other Unfinished.

"Let's go," Holly said as she stuffed some of her hair underneath her knitted cap.

They hopped on the Turapids and held their brushes tightly. Holly noticed that an orange spot had lit up in the lake just like the squares in the Aqua-inking pool. She zoomed past Brian and touched the spot right on time. A "ping" sounded from the island.

"That was the first point," she said, excited.

Brian and Amanda shot back and forth, trying to catch the squares that lit up. Amanda hit three squares in a row, and Brian got five.

"I didn't know you could be so good," Holly yelled across the lake to Brian. "See what you can do if you focus on the game?"

"Stop them," echoed across the lake again.

Holly, Brian, and Amanda halted their Turapids. Five Unfinished stood behind them back at the gate to the foggy hall. Their hoods were pulled down, and their pencil outlines whirled around in rage. They growled and jumped on a few Turapids.

"I think we have a problem now," Amanda said.

"Get out of the way," said Brian, shooting off into the

distance.

One monk maneuvered his Turapid toward Holly. The other Unfinished spread out across the lake, chasing after Amanda and Brian.

Holly swung her brush and applied the Redirection Brushstroke. A thread of paint shot toward the monk. He veered around and pointed his brush at her.

Holly halted abruptly, and the thread of titanium-white paint missed her by a few inches. A pink square lit up some feet away. She zoomed over and touched it. A gong echoed from the island. The box at the gate of the annex had opened up.

Relieved, Holly smiled. "The box is open!" she shouted.

They had achieved their goal and they could head to the island now.

Amanda was speeding between two Unfinished. She passed one of the lit-up squares, the Unfinished following close behind her.

Just as she approached the island, Brian shot in between and yelled, "Unfinished are scum!"

The monks turned away from Amanda and pursued Brian. He zoomed across the lake away from the island, the monks trailing behind him.

"Get to the island and open the gate. I'll distract them," called Brian as he zoomed by Holly. He held out his brush over his shoulder and made the Redirection Brushstroke. His paint knocked an Unfinished off his Turapid.

Holly made a wide circle and headed for the island. One of the Unfinished noticed and chased after her. She halted abruptly, aimed her brush, and made the Redirection Brushstroke. The

thread of paint hit the Unfinished right on the chest. He tumbled, spun around, and shot off into the distance.

Far away, Brian was yelling all kinds of insults at the Unfinished. Holly was just a few feet away from the island. The Turapid halted, and she hopped onto the rocky beach. Amanda was waiting for her at the gate.

"Open it!" said Holly. "We don't have any time to lose."

Amanda hurled the golden brush into the box. It spun in a circle and turned into a fire wheel that blasted sparks in all directions. When the sparks subsided, a color wheel appeared.

"What's going on now?" asked Amanda, staring at the wheel, surprised. "It should open the gate."

Holly shook her head and waited. But nothing happened. Then she remembered what the abbot had said.

"When you get to the Golden Maple Tree, match the color of the entrance to the color wheel. Otherwise the island will sink," Holly said.

"What?" Amanda asked.

"That's what the abbot said. Remember? We didn't know what he meant then."

Holly stepped up to the color wheel and selected gold. As in Color Painting I, the wheel spun around and a selection of different types of gold appeared. Holly matched the color of the gate to one of the swatches and touched it. Nine golden squares appeared. They all looked identical.

"Hurry up," Brian shouted in the distance.

Holly and Amanda turned back to the lake.

"Jeepers," said Holly.

Brian was speeding over the lake. Dozens of Unfinished

had joined the monks in chasing him. Each second, another Unfinished appeared from the fog and mounted a Turapid.

"You have to do this, Amanda," said Holly, pointing at the color wheel. "I can't see a difference between these colors."

Amanda eyed the colors carefully. "I'm not really sure. It is either this one or that one." She pointed at two swatches in the upper row. Amanda bit her nails. "I just don't know."

"I can't redirect them much longer," shouted Brian across the lake. "Open that gate now."

Holly squinted and focused on the golden swatches, but she didn't see the difference.

"I have an idea," said Amanda.

She swung her brush and used the Cannon Brushstroke to carve out a tiny piece of gold from the gate. Just as the tiny nugget was about to shoot away into the distance, Amanda caught it with her hand. She held the nugget directly next to the two swatches.

"It's the left one," said Amanda. "Now I can see it clearly."

Holly touched the left swatch, and the island rumbled as if an earthquake were shaking it.

"Are you sure it was the correct one?" Holly asked.

Amanda looked scared, but didn't say a word.

The island shook once again, and the gate gradually opened up. A long tunnel was ahead of them. At the end of the tunnel Holly could see the moon shining down on something she had been hoping to find for a long time.

"Jeepers. There it is," said Holly. "The Golden Maple Tree."

The Golden Maple Tree

Whether books, paintings, movies, or games, they all have the power to take you to a world of fantasy.

The Golden Maple Tree was shimmering in the moonlight. Its branches were of pure gold, and high up on the trunk Holly could see little windows and ladders. It was as if someone was living inside.

"Run!" Brian shouted from far away across the lake.

Holly spun around and saw Brian approaching. The Unfinished pursued him, brushes held high above their heads and firing like machine guns.

"Go!" Brian yelled.

"We can't leave you behind," Holly yelled. "Hurry up!"

"You have to save Rufus and Ileana," shouted Brian while coming closer. "Get to the tree."

Holly nodded reluctantly. She ran through the tunnel toward the Golden Maple Tree. As she reached the end of the tunnel, the gate behind them rumbled again.

"It's closing!" said Amanda, throwing her hands over her mouth. "What are we going to do? Brian won't be able to get in."

Holly saw Brian approaching the gate, but just before he reached it, the doors closed with a loud bang.

"It's too late," Holly said as her stomach turned. She felt sick. What would happen to Brian now?

She spun around to the Golden Maple Tree. It was surrounded by arcades of columns. A fountain bubbled in each corner of the courtyard. The tree's branches reached far above the walls. The sky was black with squawking creatures that circled the treetop.

"Chandrills," said Amanda. "There are thousands." She pointed at a branch. "Look."

A bright green leaf was emerging among the golden leaves. It grew rapidly and, in front of their eyes, folded up to form a Chandrill. The leaf began to squawk and tore itself off the branch. As the creature fluttered up into the sky to join the others, another flock swooped down to the courtyard. They nestled in the low-hanging branches of the tree. Suddenly, millions of Giraflies emerged from the Chandrills and assembled in the courtyard in the form of two giraffes.

"So that's how the Chandrills grow," Holly said.

"We have to get some leaves," said Amanda. She darted into the courtyard toward the tree. As she reached for a branch, a flock of Chandrills in the tree swooped down on her.

"Get out of there," Holly shouted. "They're attacking!"

But it was too late. The Chandrills had already surrounded Amanda and were pecking at her head. She screamed as blood dripped down her face. Her screams grew fainter as she sank to the ground and lay motionless. Holly bolted forward, her brush held out, and used the Redirection Brushstroke over and over. The Chandrills were catapulted into the distance by Holly's threads of paint. She ran to Amanda.

A rustling came from above. She glanced into the sky. The Chandrills whirled around and shot down to the courtyard again. Holly put Amanda's arm around her shoulder and dragged her behind a fountain underneath the columns.

"You'll be safe here," Holly said.

Amanda opened her eyes slightly. "Get the leaves and destroy the tree," she barely breathed the words. "Don't worry about me."

"I'll never be able to get to the tree with all the Chandrills in the courtyard," said Holly. "But let's see if my Creation and Deletion studies have paid off." She swung her brush and painted a rectangle with a few curved lines inside.

A bucket with some liquid formed in the air and set down on the ground. Holly dipped her finger inside and licked it. "Yes. It worked," she said.

"What are you doing?" asked Amanda, propping herself up on the stone floor.

"Chandrills don't attack Giraflies," Holly said. "If Giraflies are like regular flies, they will love sweets. This is honey. If I pour it over myself and get the Giraflies to cover me, the Chandrills might not attack, just like they didn't attack Ms.

Hubbleworth."

Holly lifted up the bucket and poured the honey over her head. It dripped off her knitted cap and down onto her face. She approached the giraffes. The Giraflies shot toward her. Holly took a deep breath and closed her eyes. She was afraid of what would happen next but tried to stay calm. A second later, the Giraflies were crawling all over her body. Holly felt a tingling sensation as if she were being massaged from head to toe.

She reached out to one of the low-hanging branches. The moment she touched the branch, it pulled away from her. The Giraflies dispersed in all directions and Holly opened her eyes just in time to see the branch swinging at her. It slapped her right in the face. Holly tumbled to the ground. But she got back up and tried it a second time.

"What do you want?" a deep male voice boomed.

"Who's speaking?" Holly asked.

"I am—the tree house."

"A tree house?" asked Holly, surprised. "I live in one."

The Golden Maple Tree twisted its trunk, and a thick pair of lips appeared in the wood. The lips opened up and a voice came out. "I'm Villa Maplethorn. What tree house do you live in?"

"I live in Villa Nonesuch. She's my friend."

The thick lips smiled. "Villa Nonesuch? She's a distant relative of mine."

Holly stepped closer to the trunk.

A pair of tiny green eyes stared at her. "And who are you?"

"I'm Holly O'Flanigan. Could you please give me some of your leaves? I've heard they can cure people. My friend Ileana is really sick and she needs them."

"So you are the Gindar who everybody is talking about," said the Golden Maple Tree. "I have heard about you. Cuspidor is afraid of you. You are the only one who can destroy him." The tiny eyes squinted.

"That's a bit too much," said Holly. "I doubt that Cuspidor is afraid of me."

"Come in. But first let's get rid of those nasty Giraflies." A few branches brushed past her, got rid of the remaining flies, and wiped Holly clean with their leaves. The mouth on the trunk turned into a door and sprang open.

"Can I get my friend Amanda?" asked Holly. "She was attacked by the Chandrills."

"Go ahead," said Villa Maplethorn. "I'll keep the Chandrills at bay."

Holly ran across the courtyard, helped Amanda up, and dragged her over to the door of the tree house. The Chandrills squawked terribly as Villa Maplethorn hit them with his branches.

Holly and Amanda stumbled inside the tree house. The door closed behind them and dissolved into the wall. The squawking of the Chandrills stopped.

"We really don't have much time," said Holly, staring at an empty room, which looked like a storage place for piles of straw. "We need to find Ileana and Rufus. Ms. Hubbleworth has kidnapped them."

"Was that the old lady in pink with the sunhat?" Villa

Maplethorn asked.

"You've seen her?" asked Holly, leading Amanda to a pile of straw.

"Yes, she entered the Hall of Fears," said the tree house.

"The Hall of Fears?" Holly didn't like the sound of it. "Why is it called that way?"

"It used to be a torture room hundreds of years ago," Villa Maplethorn said. "The old lady wasn't alone. She had two children tied to her griffin."

"Rufus and Ileana," Amanda whispered.

"Can you show me where they went?" Holly asked.

Villa Maplethorn twisted his walls, and a door appeared on the opposite side from where they had entered. The door flew open.

"Ms. Hubbleworth went into the backyard," Villa Maplethorn said.

Holly stepped out. She was surrounded on all sides by a high sandstone wall. Opposite her, a stone head of a giant seahorse protruded from the wall. Its mouth was an entrance.

"This is the entrance to the Hall of Fears," said Villa Maplethorn. "It leads to Cuspidor's castle."

"Can Amanda stay here until I get back?" Holly asked.

"Of course," said Villa Maplethorn, flapping the door. "But don't forget the leaves." A branch swung in front of the door, and two golden leaves sailed to the ground. "Give one to Amanda, and keep one for Ileana."

Holly went back inside and kneeled down next to Amanda. She rubbed the leaf against Amanda's face but nothing happened.

"You might have to eat it," said Holly. "Just ask Villa Maplethorn." She placed the leaf in Amanda's hand. "I'll be back soon."

Amanda nodded and propped herself up. "I want to come with you."

"No. You have to recover first," Holly said.

She headed for the seahorse's mouth. As she got closer she noticed sweat dripping into her eyes. She wiped it off with her sleeve. What was she going to find in there? She grabbed her paintbrush tightly and stepped closer. The beat of her heart sounded so loud that she could hardly hear the squawking of the Chandrills above. She briefly looked back and saw the door of Villa Maplethorn vanish into the bark. The branches above her flapped around, protecting her from the Chandrills.

Holly opened the door in the seahorse's mouth and stepped inside. It was dark. Only the moonlight from behind lit the hall. Carved seahorses decorated the arches that spanned a half circle staircase in the center. It only had ten steps, leading up to a tunnel.

On the top few stairs, right in front of the tunnel, was a statue.

Holly illuminated her brush. Bright colors of mosaics on the steps became visible. She flinched in surprise. That wasn't a statue sitting on the stairs. It was Ms. Hubbleworth. Her eyes were closed and her mouth was wide open as if she were unconscious. Next to her was another person.

"Rufus!" Holly shouted.

Rufus' hands were tied, and his mouth gagged. He shook his head while trying to scream.

"Let me take that off," said Holly, approaching the staircase.

Rufus violently shook his head. "Gontcumkous," he said.

"What?" Holly asked, climbing the stairs.

A shadow of a person appeared in the tunnel. "Rufus said, 'Don't come close.' But it's too late now," said the shadow.

The Hall of Fears

You will never really know what reality is and what it is not because reality is in the eye of the beholder.

Holly stopped on the stairs, still holding her illuminated brush. A thread of paint shot out of the dark and hit her arm. She dropped the brush. The light went out.

"You shouldn't have come," said the person in the tunnel.

Holly's eyes slowly adjusted to the dim lighting. The person stepped out of the darkness.

"Ileana," said Holly, gaping at her friend. "Is that you?"

Ileana's face had completely dissolved into pencil lines. All that was left of the friend Holly had once known were a few strands of hair.

"I thought she kidnapped you," Holly said, pointing at the motionless Ms. Hubbleworth on the stairs. "What's wrong with her?"

In slow motion, Holly bent down to pick up her brush. Ileana didn't react.

Just then, a sizzling sound filled the air, and four seahorses shot out of the tunnel. Ileana turned her head. Holly used this distraction to pick up her brush and hide it in her pocket.

The seahorses spat fire and forced Ileana aside. A giant black shadow appeared in the tunnel.

Holly's heart turned into a knot and she bit her lip.

Cuspidor stepped out of the tunnel. A black cloak covered his entire body, and a hood was pulled over his face.

"Why are you covering yourself?" shouted Holly. "I know what you are."

"Yes, why should I?" Cuspidor said.

He flipped his hood back and hurled the cloak over his shoulder. Holly was shocked. She had expected nothing but pencil lines, but she was mistaken. Last year Cuspidor's feet and calves were the only parts of his body that had been completed. This time he was finished up to his hips.

A shiver went down her spine.

"I'm glad my plan to bring you here worked," Cuspidor said.

"I came here by my own choice," said Holly, clenching her fists.

"No, you wouldn't be here if I hadn't planned for you to come," said Cuspidor, laughing loudly. "You found the monastery only because I wanted you to find it."

"I found the painting in the Gallery of Wonders all by myself," Holly said.

"No, you didn't," said Cuspidor, laughing devilishly. "The Q woman helped you."

Holly gaped. "You mean she had something to do with you?"

"Of course," explained Cuspidor. "After last year's events, LePawnee guarded you so well that I would have never gotten hold of you. So I had to lure you out of Magora." He stepped down the stairs.

Holly backed off.

"Remember the day you went to Ravenscraig Lane to look for the Momarian Hell Library?"

Holly nodded.

"You went to Patwood Bookstore. The Hissler you met is one of my people and was supposed to feed you this news."

"That was planned?" Holly asked, surprised.

"Of course. The Hissler had to give you the cube with the Q woman inside. But since you gave him the correct change, he had to lower his price for the book in order to give you the Q I wanted you to have. The book was empty from the beginning. It was only a hook to give you the Q."

Rufus managed to pull down the gag with his shoulder. "Let me go," he shouted, trying to free himself.

Rufus turned his head to Holly. "It wasn't Ms. Hubbleworth who did all this. It was Cuspidor inside her body. He found Hubbleworth's mindless body marching along the Wall of Gors last year."

Suddenly, things started to make sense to Holly. So Cuspidor had used Ms. Hubbleworth all along. Holly remembered how surprised she had been when the professor had told them about the Momarian Hell Library. She also hadn't understood why Hubbleworth had told them to steal the key from Professor LePawnee's office. But it had not been Ms. Hubbleworth after all: it was Cuspidor's mind inside her body, controlling her.

"But why did he kidnap you and Ileana?" Holly asked.

"He found out that we were doing the blood experiment in Farouche's class," said Rufus. "He wanted your blood that I had collected in the tube, but I refused to give it to him. So he thought I was a good hostage to lure you here."

Finally Holly understood the connection. Not only did Rufus have her blood in the tubes, Ileana also had Holly's blood as well. It was running in Ileana's veins because of Holly's blood transfusions.

"You only wanted my blood," said Holly. "You didn't care about Ileana or Rufus."

Cuspidor laughed. "You are a little slow, but you've finally managed to put two and two together. Because of them I'm in better shape than ever." He pointed at his finished lower body. "Enough talk." Cuspidor pulled a brush out of his cloak pocket.

Holly was prepared to fight. She was about to take out her brush when someone tapped her on the shoulder.

"Don't you even think about attacking him," said Ileana, holding her brush directly at Holly's left temple. She laughed maniacally as the pencil lines in her face whirled around.

"Ileana," said Holly. "Try to remember who you were. You wouldn't do this to me."

"Quiet!" shouted Ileana, poking her brush deep into Holly's skin.

Holly leaned her head to the other side, trying to avoid the brush. "I'm your friend."

Ileana gave Holly a push. At that precise moment, Cuspidor aimed and shot at Holly. As if a stone had hit her in the chest, Holly stumbled backward. Ileana jumped out of her way. A thread of titanium white paint hovered between Holly and Cuspidor's brush. It began to darken with red. Holly felt nauseated and tumbled to the ground.

"Ileana," she said. "Help me. Remember who you are."

Ileana leaned over her, hungrily sniffing Holly's blood that crawled along the thread of paint.

"Remember the first time we went to the bakery?" Holly asked. "We bought marzipan griffins together. Try to remember that."

But Ileana didn't seem to hear anything. She kept sniffing the blood like a vulture its carrion.

Holly's mind wandered. She thought of the Griffin Hatchery, Whitespot, and Cookie. If the troll were here, he would help her. But Cookie didn't even know where she was. There was nobody but Amanda and Brian left. Amanda was injured, and Brian might have been overpowered by the Unfinished.

Cuspidor's voice began to hammer in her head. At the end of last school year he had almost killed her, draining her blood. But this year Holly was more prepared. She had practiced many protection brushstrokes and she knew what Cuspidor had planned: like all Unfinished he would try to talk to her and distract her so that she would want to give up fighting. She would not let him do that again.

Brian is dead, Cuspidor's voice echoed in her mind. *Give up.*

There's no way out.

"You are not going to distract me this time," Holly propped herself up. "You have tricked me so many times—why should I believe anything you say?"

Holly pulled out her brush. But she felt too weak to point it at Cuspidor. She dropped her arm to her side, holding the brush lightly in her fist as her blood kept running through the thread of paint. When it reached Cuspidor, he breathed heavily as if a burst of energy penetrated his whole body.

Ileana was prancing up and down the thread of paint, still sniffing the blood.

What about your father? Cuspidor asked.

Holly's focus shifted to Cuspidor. "What about my father? He died in an accident, just like my mother."

Did he? Cuspidor asked. *What if I told you that your father is alive?*

"Liar!" shouted Holly. "If he were alive, he wouldn't have left me with the Smoralls."

Holly loosened the grip on the brush. Her father was dead. She knew it. Cuspidor was just trying to distract her. She had to focus.

Ileana dipped her tongue into the thread of paint and licked some of Holly's blood.

"Out of the way," Cuspidor shouted angrily at Ileana.

Ileana stepped closer to Holly until she was just a hand's width away from her.

Holly saw Ileana's unfinished head. A sudden idea shot through her mind. Hadn't Farouche mentioned in his class that Unfinished wore each other out when fighting for blood?

What if Ileana attacked Cuspidor?

Holly whispered, "Ileana, Cuspidor is stealing blood from you, keeping you from becoming finished. Are you going to let him do that?"

Ileana's pencil lines whirled around. She turned toward Cuspidor.

"Get the blood from him," Holly said.

Ileana pointed her brush and shot at Cuspidor. A thread of white paint hit his right thigh and blood started to crawl toward Ileana.

Cuspidor roared. His cloak fluttered in the air as he spun around. The stream of paint draining from Holly halted, and she felt blood rushing back into all her veins at once. It was like breathing for the first time again after having held her breath for minutes. She propped herself up and crawled toward Rufus.

A new thread of paint shot out of Cuspidor's brush and hit Ileana. The blood crawled back and forth between the two while Holly untied Rufus.

She briefly looked at Ms. Hubbleworth, but she seemed frozen like a statue.

"Is she still alive?" Holly asked.

"I have no idea," Rufus said. "She froze when we got here and has not blinked once since then."

"All right," whispered Holly. "I have an idea how we can scare Cuspidor away."

"How?" Rufus asked.

"I'll tell you later. Stay here and wait until I shout your name," said Holly. "Then try to knock Ileana to the ground."

Rufus nodded.

She tiptoed unnoticed past Cuspidor and Ileana and back through the entrance door. When she came out, she spotted Amanda standing in front of Villa Maplethorn.

"You're all right," Holly said as she ran to Amanda and hugged her.

"The leaf worked," Amanda said.

"We have to hurry," said Holly. "I need you to do something very important."

Holly swung her brush and created one of the magic balloons she had mistaken for a sun during the Christmas party. She handed it to Amanda.

"When I say 'now,' let the balloon go," Holly said.

Amanda nodded.

Holly ran back to the Hall of Fears, entered, and closed the door behind her. Once inside, she stomped on the ground.

"Didn't you notice that I escaped?" she yelled at Cuspidor and Ileana.

The two dropped their brushes and stared at Holly for a few seconds in disbelief. Then, Cuspidor growled and leaped forward.

"Rufus. Now!" Holly yelled.

Rufus leaped down from the stairs, knocked Ileana to the ground, and twisted her arm behind her back.

Holly swung her brush. A thread shot toward Cuspidor and hit the pencil lines that suggested where his eyes would be.

"What have you done?" he screamed. "Everything is blurry."

"It's just something I've learned when studying healing

brushstrokes," said Holly. "It numbs your vision. I bet you can't see me all that well anymore." She laughed, dashed to the door, and yanked it open.

"Now," she said when she saw Amanda outside.

Amanda let go of the balloon, which rose up and brightened the sky. It glittered between the branches of Villa Maplethorn.

"Sunlight," said Holly, pointing high up into the tree. "Morning has arrived. Now you will fade."

Cuspidor threw his arms into the air and screamed, "I will be back, Holly O'Flanigan and then I will drain every drop of blood from you!" He flung his cloak over his head and escaped up the stairs and into the tunnel.

Cuspidor was gone.

Holly ran to Rufus who was sitting on Ileana's back, holding his paintbrush to her head.

Ileana's pencil lines whirled rapidly around and she growled. Holly shoved the golden leaf into her open mouth.

Ileana fell silent.

Who is Who?

Magic only lasts as long as a fantasy world doesn't become everyday life. When routine takes over, the magic pops like a balloon in a fire.

Rufus loosened his grip on Ileana as some of her holes began to close.

"I think it is working," Rufus said.

Holly felt a sudden burst of energy and excitement flooding her body. All her efforts had paid off. Ileana would survive. "It helped Amanda," said Holly. "I hope it will cure Ileana fully."

"Yes, it really helped me," said Amanda, standing at the entrance to the hall.

Rufus smiled when he saw her. Amanda sped inside and hugged Rufus.

"I'm glad you're okay," said Amanda. "I was really worried."

At that moment, Holly heard a griffin squeaking at the entrance. They all went outside. A carriage pulled by six griffins landed in front of Villa Maplethorn. Professor Gobeli and Farouche stepped out. Holly and Rufus went to the carriage.

"What are you doing here?" Holly asked, relieved.

"Holly!" yelled Brian, jumping out of the carriage. "Are you all right? I'm so glad you didn't get hurt."

Two more griffins landed next to the carriage. Professor LePawnee dismounted from her griffin, while Cookie climbed down from the other.

"Cookie!" Holly jumped at the troll's neck. "I'm so glad to see you here."

The shape-shifter hugged her and smiled.

"They saved my life," said Brian. "The Unfinished were about to catch me when Cookie and the professors appeared and stopped them."

"We freed the monks in the dungeon, and the abbot told us where you were," said LePawnee. "Some of them are already back to work." She pointed to the tree top.

Five monks were sitting on the branches, diligently cutting off the budding leaves.

"From now on there won't be any Chandrills," Cookie said.

"Where did the other Chandrills go?" asked Holly, searching the sky for a sign of the flocks that had attacked Amanda.

"My bats had babies a week ago. Now they outnumbered the Chandrills," said Gobeli, pointing at a pile of leaves on the ground. "And since the Chandrills couldn't reproduce anymore, my bats were done with them in no time."

"Professor Hubbleworth is still inside," said Holly. "She's not really responsive."

"I'll take care of her," LePawnee said.

She handed the leash of her griffin to Gobeli and headed inside the Hall of Fears. Cookie, Gobeli, and Farouche saddled up on two griffins.

"I guess you don't need us anymore, so we'll be heading back to Cliffony," Professor Farouche said.

All three of them took off into the sky. Holly waved.

"Thank you," she called.

Just as they were about to go back inside the Hall of Fears, Holly heard the flapping of wings above.

"Are they coming back?" Brian asked.

A griffin swooped down and landed in front of the carriage. Holly rubbed her eyes in disbelief. A woman she knew very well was sitting on the griffin. It was Professor Hubbleworth.

"How can that be?" Rufus asked. "Professor Hubbleworth is in there." He pointed at the mouth of the giant seahorse that led into the Hall of Fears.

Holly did not understand. She had seen Professor Hubbleworth on the stairs just a few moments ago. But now she was seeing her sitting on the griffin. She was wearing the same ugly sunhat, the same thick makeup, and the same pink dress.

"I guess I'm a bit too late to help," the professor said. "I was visiting my cousin when I got the news. It took me a while to get here."

Holly looked from Hubbleworth to Brian and Amanda. They looked utterly confused.

"Maybe she has a twin," Brian whispered.

As Professor Hubbleworth dismounted the griffin, a squawk echoed from above. The nasty macaw swooped down and pulled two strands of Holly's hair.

Holly winced swatted her hand at the bird to ward it off. It spun in a circle and landed on the ground.

As if the parrot had just noticed something, it wobbled straight into the Hall of Fears. Brian and Amanda followed.

Holly turned to Professor Hubbleworth. "Could you wait here for a second?" she asked.

Holly wanted to see the other Hubbleworth again. She went inside and closed the door behind her.

Inside, bright light illuminated the interior of the Hall of Fears. Professor LePawnee had created a few torches and was standing on the staircase next to Professor Hubbleworth's twin.

The macaw suddenly swung itself up into the air and squawked loudly. It circled Ms. Hubbleworth's body a few times. Then, it dropped to the ground as if it had been shot.

Holly went over and touched it. The parrot was dead.

What was going on? Holly didn't understand why the bird had just died. It had been chasing after Hubbleworth for months, and now all of a sudden it died without having shown any sign of weakness before. And to top it all off, there was a second Hubbleworth waiting outside the Hall of Fears.

A humming sounded behind Holly. She turned back. As if hit by a stun gun, Ms. Hubbleworth's lifeless body shook and she began to cough. Her eyes opened.

"What happened?" she said, turning to Professor LePawnee.

"You again? You left us behind in the dunes."

"Are you all right?" LePawnee asked.

Ms. Hubbleworth jumped up as she saw Holly. "Nothing is all right. A moment ago, I was in Donkleywood and then I fell into that hole up in the attic and ended up in this strange world, and now I'm—" She looked around, confused. "Where am I?"

It seemed that Ms. Hubbleworth's last memory was of when she had crossed the Wall of Gors a year ago.

Suddenly, everything made sense to Holly. She ran to the entrance and peeked out.

"Thank you so much for your help, Professor. Professor LePawnee says she doesn't need you anymore. You can go back to your cousin now," she said, slamming the door shut in front of the second Hubbleworth's face. Holly went back to her friends, while LePawnee swung her brush over Ms. Hubbleworth's body, healing a few scratches.

"I think I know what happened," Holly said. "Remember last year when we first came to Magora?"

Her friends nodded, and Professor LePawnee said, "Of course, I welcomed you here and took you across Lake Santima."

"After you left," Holly said to LePawnee, "Ms. Hubbleworth took Mind-Splitting Powder and wandered off into the distance without really knowing how the powder worked. The most important rule of MSP is that you focus on your body so that your mind can reunite with it behind the Wall of Gors. But Ms. Hubbleworth didn't know about that, so she never did that."

Brian's mouth dropped open. "You mean that Ms.

Hubbleworth's mind never returned to her body?"

"Not to the same body," said Amanda. "The Gors must have caught a parrot and drained its mind, and then Ms. Hubbleworth's mind entered the parrot's body."

"Something like that can happen when a mind can't find its body," LePawnee said as she walked toward the exit. "I'll get the griffins so that we can go back to Cliffony." She stepped outside.

Holly turned to her friends, while Ms. Hubbleworth stared at the ground, muttering to herself.

"Cuspidor found Ms. Hubbleworth's empty body," said Holly. "As an Unfinished he was able to use it and pretend to be Professor Hubbleworth."

"Yes," said Amanda. "And the parrot knew that Cuspidor was in her body. So it attacked him."

"All this sounds great, but haven't you overlooked a tiny little detail?" Rufus asked.

"What?" Brian asked.

"There is a second Hubbleworth out there," Rufus said.

Holly smiled. "Don't you get it?" she asked.

"Get what?" Rufus asked.

"Grandpa Nikolas based Magora and its people on real life," said Holly. "He had known Ms. Hubbleworth in Donkleywood for a long time. When he painted Magora, he found inspiration in the real world. So he copied Ms. Hubbleworth's image to create one of the professors at Cliffony."

"This is confusing," Amanda said.

"Remember, this Ms. Hubbleworth—" Holly pointed at the muttering old lady in front of them, "—did not know anything

about Magora. She entered this world with us last year. The Professor Hubbleworth we saw all year, however, was teaching Gate Paintings at Cliffony. She did not know anything about Donkleywood—because she had never been there."

Amanda, Brian, and Rufus stared at Holly with shocked looks on their faces.

"There's a Hubbleworth in Donkleywood and there's one in Magora," Holly concluded. "And each one has her own separate life."

Brian looked flabbergasted. "So you 're saying there are copies of some people in Donkleywood living here in Magora?"

Holly nodded. "Remember when you thought you saw your mother in Ravenscraig Lane?"

"Yes," said Brian. "You mean she was a copy of my mom in Donkleywood?"

"That would make sense," said Amanda, turning to Holly. "And you saw Ms. Smorall. She was probably a double as well."

Rufus looked somewhat pale. He breathed heavily. "B-b-but," he stuttered, "if there is a copy of Ms. Smorall and of Brian's mother, then there could also be—"

He trembled and sat down on the stairs.

"What? Amanda asked.

"There could be doubles of all of us," he said.

There was silence.

Holly hadn't thought of that. Could it be that she had a twin here in Magora as well?

"There wouldn't be a double of me," said Amanda. "I

didn't even know Grandpa Nikolas. He couldn't have copied me."

"I doubt that we all have copies," said Brian. "If there were any, we would have already met them."

Holly nodded. But deep inside, she hoped that there were copies of everybody. Then she might get the chance to see Grandpa Nikolas and her parents again.

Family

Escaping into other worlds is a refreshing experience, but it can also be dangerous. Once you have decided to stay in this new world, fantasy becomes reality. Then the door back to reality has been closed forever.

A day later, Holly woke up in Villa Nonesuch. It was the day of their return to Donkleywood. Even though it had been a dangerous year again, she dreaded the idea of living with the Smoralls, even if it was just for the summer vacation. She hugged Tenshi, went to the bathroom, and got dressed. When she walked down the stairs, the room was filled with people. Cookie and Professor LePawnee were chatting in the kitchen, while the Ms. Hubbleworth from Donkleywood was sitting in the recliner, mumbling to herself.

Gobeli and Farouche carried a large painting inside the tree house. They leaned it against the wall.

Holly looked at the gray buildings in the picture. She really didn't want to go back to Donkleywood, but she knew she had to in order not to raise suspicion in the town. Otherwise, someone might discover that they were not going to boarding school in Bitterfield.

"Are you ready?" Amanda said, coming down the stairs with Rufus.

Holly's mouth dropped open.

"What happened to your hair?" she asked.

Amanda had a buzz haircut. She ran her red fingernails through it.

"Don't you think it looks sassy?" She turned on the spot, showing all sides of her hair. "That experience with the Chandrills did it for me," she said. "When they started pulling out my hair, I promised myself I would cut it."

Brian came running down the stairs after Amanda.

"Wow," he said. "Last year I thought your hair was short, but now this is really short. You look a little boyish now."

"That's why I used a bolder color lipstick," said Amanda, pointing at her bright red lips. "I created it myself." She grabbed Brian and kissed the back of his hand. "There, you can see the color even better."

Brian pulled his hand back. He grimaced and wiped his hand on his pants.

"I think you look great, Amanda," Holly said, laughing.

"I think it is time to go now," Cookie said, his head drooping.

"Don't worry," Holly said, giving the shape-shifter a kiss on his big nose. "We'll be back in a couple of months."

Holly said goodbye to the professors. Then she turned back to Professor LePawnee.

"What's going to happen to the monastery?" Holly asked.

"We have secured it," said Professor LePawnee. "The monks will resume harvesting the Golden Maple Tree. No more Chandrills will bud from now on."

A pecking on the window made Holly turn. Rufus opened it with a smile. Shardee fluttered in.

"How is Shardee still alive?" Holly asked, as the creature landed on Rufus' shoulder.

"I don't know," said Professor LePawnee. "He should have died last winter if he were a true Chandrill."

Holly smiled. Whatever kind of creature he was, she was glad that Shardee had turned out to be a true friend for Rufus.

"Are you ready?" Cookie interrupted, a tear running down his cheek. "I will miss you."

Holly smiled. "I will miss you, too. But I'll be back soon."

"I do have some good news," said Professor Kaplin. "Ileana has stabilized. By the time you're back next fall, she should be her normal self again."

Holly smiled. Even though she was sad that they had to leave, a feeling of satisfaction and happiness rose within her. They had saved Ileana.

Professor LePawnee swung her brush. Bright lights emanated from the painting. The gate to Donkleywood was open.

"Time to go," said the professor.

"Wait," a voice came from outside. Marvin bolted in.

Holly twitched, while everybody else turned to the door.

Had something dangerous happened again? Holly feared that Marvin was bringing news that Cuspidor was back already.

But instead Marvin smiled as he unfolded a paper. "I have the results from the experiment in Unfinished Painting II," he said. "Holly has the largest amount of Gindar acrylans in her blood. Gina only came in second."

"Really?" Holly couldn't believe it. So she was more of a Gindar than Gina after all.

Marvin handed Holly the results. Then he grabbed her by the shoulders and gave her a kiss on the cheek. "Goodbye," he said.

Before Holly even realized what had happened, Marvin had already spun around and shot out of the room.

For a moment, Holly felt embarrassed, but then she was really glad she had met Marvin, even though he was living in a fantasy world.

"Are you ready now?" LePawnee asked, pointing at the open gate.

Cookie squatted down next to Holly, wiped some fluff off Holly's sweater, and stroked her hair away from her face. "Be careful. And don't let the Smoralls push you around too much." He sighed. "And comb your hair sometimes, and don't forget to—"

"I will, Dad," said Holly, absentmindedly.

"Dad?" Cookie asked with a smile on his face.

"Oh, I'm sorry, I-I-I," stuttered Holly. "I didn't mean to—"

"That's all right," said the shape-shifter, taking Holly in his arms. "You can call me Dad anytime you want."

Holly kissed Cookie on the cheek. Then she turned to the painting of Donkleywood and stepped closer. She peered over her shoulder at Cookie and said, "Goodbye." With a smile she added, "Dad."

Then she stepped into the lights.

TURN THE PAGE FOR A GLIMPSE
INTO HOLLY'S NEXT JOURNEY IN

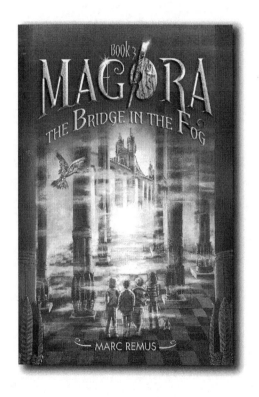

BOOK 3 - THE BRIDGE IN FOG

Fog

I have often wondered what creativity might be. It is a strange phenomenon. It comes and goes and never stays for long.

The somber growling of cloaked creatures echoed as Holly wandered aimlessly through an ocean of fog. Each time a howl sounded, she threw herself to the ground, curling up so that she remained hidden from the evil Unfinished that filled the area.

She heard a scuffing sound nearby. "Brian," whispered Holly. "Where are you?"

But all she heard in reply was another nearby growl. Brian was nowhere to be seen. Would Holly ever find him? Would they get out? She followed the dim rays of light that flickered through the mist. Looking up, she saw a giant bridge towering above her.

"I'm back at the bridge," she mumbled. "I keep walking in circles. I wonder—"

A roar interrupted Holly. She spun around and stared into the face of something she couldn't define. It was one of the Unfinished. The face was made up of pencil lines that hovered in the air. Scattered pieces of flesh swirled in between the lines as the face let out a piercing scream.

Holly turned and darted into the fog. She didn't get far. Another Unfinished blocked her way. She veered around and shot in another direction.

"Brian! Brian!" she shouted.

But there was no sign of him anywhere.

Out of nowhere a strange creature appeared, but this time it wasn't an Unfinished. It was a boy who was made out of pine cones. For hair he had pine needles, and his eyes were tiny bright green pine cones. He smiled.

"Thank you, Holly," said the boy in a calm voice. Then he vanished.

Holly was about to run away when the fog vanished for a moment and the courtyard of a monastery became visible. An ornate golden gate decorated with angels, peacocks, and elves was in front of her.

As suddenly as the fog had disappeared, it returned.

Panicked, Holly took the last path of escape that had not been blocked. But a giant double-headed Unfinished suddenly appeared out of nowhere and ended that plan. She was

surrounded. There was no way out.

"Move aside," rasped a voice. "She's mine."

Another cloaked figure appeared, his paintbrush held high. He swung it, and a stream of white paint shot out, hitting Holly on the chest. She screamed, dropped to the ground, and shook a few times. Then she was still.

Marc Remus is an award-winning German Neo Pop-Art painter and illustrator with exhibitions world-wide. He was educated in the United States, graduated with a BA in art and illustration from Art Center College of Design in Pasadena, CA, and lived in Japan and Central America for some years. He has travelled to more than sixty countries and visited over a thousand cities, of which he has painted over two hundred. His work has been featured on TV and in many magazines and newspapers in Germany, USA, and Mexico.

During his studies in California, Remus took his first children's book illustration class. His teacher inspired him to start writing and not just illustrating. The result was a picture book called *Painting Brian*, which led to the *Magora* series. Over a period of twenty years, Remus has developed this magical world based on places he has visited, people he has met, and things he has learned through his studies in acting, cultural Anthropology, and linguistics.

He continues to have painting exhibitions, studies Mandarin and Spanish, and enjoys travelling the world.

Visit the website and sign up to get the latest news on Magora:
www.MarcRemus.com/author

ACKNOWLEDGEMENTS

I AM GRATEFUL to Melinda Fassett-Welles for her early support, many years ago, when she introduced me to the fascinating world of children's literature. I will always remember her kindness as I made the first uncertain steps. May she rest in peace!

I wish to thank Nancy Butts for teaching me the foundation of writing and for helping me edit the series from the very beginning. She has been a bountiful treasure of knowledge and a good friend over all the years. I couldn't have done it without you!

I appreciate the meticulous reading and copyediting by Marlo Garnsworthy and the eagle eye of Crystal Watanabe. You made the series shine.

Many people were involved with the series, though not directly with the writing. Among them: Brian Sutow, who did a fantastic job recording the first three chapters for the audio book; Jun Park, who created a stunning intro animation; Patrick Rundblad for creating the magical soundtrack for the website; Morten Gulliksen for breathing life into Tenshi.

I am grateful to the many friends who read versions of this book as it was taking shape. Damaris not only gave a character her name but also offered me much-needed advice on an early version. Dave kindly read and responded to this volume, which helped improve the book tremendously.

Elisabeth, Katja, and Sylke read this volume and gave me helpful feedback. I appreciate your support.

I wish to thank the many kids who read the books with such enthusiasm and passion and pushed me to complete the series, among them Sofia, Gigi, and Susana.

Thanks to my parents and my entire family in the US, Germany, and France for their unshakable faith in me, and especially to my mother for reactivating her English skills to read the series.

Finally, I wish to thank Nikolas for having been a fantastic teacher so many years ago and for making Magora, its characters, and places come alive. You will always have a special place in my heart.

The first two books in the Magora series have won the following literary awards:

GOLD MEDALS:
Moonbeam Children's Book Award.
Gold medal winner in the
"Pre-Teen Fiction Ebook" category, 2016.

SILVER MEDALS:
Independent Publisher Book Award (IPPY)
Silver Medal Winner in the "Juvenile Fiction" category, 2016.

Readers' Favorite Award
Silver Medal Winner in the
"Children's Fantasy/ Sci-Fi" category, 2016

Purple Dragonfly Award
Second place in the "Middle Grade Fiction" category, 2016

FINALIST:
International Book Awards
Finalist in the "Children's Fiction" category, 2016.

National Indie Excellence Awards (NIEA)
Finalist in the "Pre-Teen Fiction" category, 2016.

NABE Pinnacle Book Achievement Award
Best book in the "Juvenile Fiction" category, Winter 2016.

Pacific Book Awards
Finalist in the "Middle Grade" category, 2016

57904506R00159

Made in the USA
Lexington, KY
27 November 2016